The Magician's Tower

The Magician's Tower

A SEQUEL TO The Wizard of Dark Street

AN OONA CRATE MYSTERY

SHAWN THOMAS ODYSSEY

EGMONT
USA
NEW YORK

EGMONT

We bring stories to life

First published by Egmont USA, 2013
443 Park Avenue South, Suite 806
New York, NY 10016

1 3 5 7 9 8 6 4 2

www.egmontusa.com
www.thewizardofdarkstreet.com

Library of Congress Cataloging-in-Publication Data

Odyssey, Shawn Thomas.
The magician's tower : a sequel to The Wizard of Dark Street /
by Shawn Thomas Odyssey.
p. cm.
Summary: Detective Oona Crate enters the Magician's Tower Contest,
a competition of dangerous tasks and obstacles that has never been won.
ISBN 978-1-60684-425-0 (hardback) — ISBN 978-1-60684-426-7 (electronic book)
[1. Contests—Fiction. 2. Wizards—Fiction. 3. Magic—Fiction. 4. Apprentices—
Fiction. 5. Orphans—Fiction. 6. Mystery and detective stories.] I. Title.
PZ7.O258Mag 2013
[Fic]—dc23
2012025081

Printed in the United States of America

For Claire, Audrey, and Jacob.

And Moonbucket . . .
who transported me into the stories.

←——————→

PROLOGUE

On the sixth of March, 1852, historian Arthur Blackstone gave the following speech to the Historical Society in New York City.

"Like the hour hand on a clock, Dark Street spins through the Drift. It spirals endlessly within the space between two worlds. At the north end of the street stands an enormous gateway, the famed Iron Gates, which open for precisely one minute every night, upon the stroke of midnight, exposing the street to New York City. At the opposite end of the street stand the equally massive Glass Gates, the gateway to the Land of Faerie, which have remained locked for hundreds of human years, and are the only things keeping the Queen of the Fay and her unspeakable army of faerie warriors from murdering us all; the gates . . . and the Wizard."

In June of 1853, Blackstone released his book *The Last Faerie Road: An Incomplete History of Dark Street*. It sold fewer than one hundred copies, and, unfortunately for Mr. Blackstone's New York publishers, no one took the book very seriously.

Fellow historians mocked the idea that such a fantastical place as Dark Street might exist at all: a place with candlestick trees and joke-telling clocks, not to mention a Museum of Magical History and a graveyard where spirits come awake in the night. The notion of a magical world so close to New York—one with a Wizard living in an enchanted manor house in the middle of the street—seemed nothing short of ridiculous to the serious scholars and scientific minds of the mid-1800s. And though Blackstone claimed that the street was filled primarily with ordinary people of no magical abilities at all, the premise was too far-fetched to be believed. The book was quickly forgotten by the academics, and would be remembered only by a handful of poets and artists, who themselves viewed the book, for the most part, as the ramblings of an overactive imagination.

On Dark Street, however, the book remained an acclaimed best seller for years to come.

CHAPTER ONE

The Party

(Sunday, August 19, 1877)

T he contest is about to begin," said the Wizard. He pointed a wrinkled finger toward the far end of the outdoor party.

A short man in a top hat slowly ascended the steps to a makeshift stage, at the rear of which stood an oddly shaped tower. Round in some sections and square in others, the tower rose like a misshapen shadow from the center of Oswald Park. The pointy pyramid at the top of the tower was scarcely visible through the misty clouds several hundred feet above. At the edge of the stage, dozens of evenly spaced tables flickered in the evening lamplight, each surrounded by flawlessly dressed party-goers.

Murmurs of polite conversation filled the night air, and thirteen-year-old Oona Crate leaned back in her seat, arms folded, lost in thought. She hardly heard her uncle's words, nor did she pay much attention to the man ascending the steps.

Of all the attendees at the party, Oona was certain that it was she alone who felt uncomfortable with the evening's festivities being located in Oswald Park. Named after Oswald the Great—the most powerful of the long-dead Magicians of Old—the enormous park was where the tragedy had happened over three years ago: the accident that had taken the lives of both Oona's mother and baby sister, leaving Oona with the grievous knowledge that it was her own misguided spell that had killed them. Ever since, the park had been a dreaded place for her. A place to avoid at all costs.

But three months ago something extraordinary had happened . . .

Fresh from the excitement of solving the most difficult case of her life—a baffling mystery involving the disappearance of her uncle, the Wizard—Oona had decided to face her fear and attend the Dark Street Annual Midnight Masquerade. It had been the first time she'd set foot on the park's grassy grounds since the day the magic had flown out of her control. It had also been the first time Oona had danced with a boy.

The night of the dance had been magical, the boy gentlemanly and handsome, and afterward, as they took their leave, she had thought that she was finally finished with her guilt over her mother's and sister's deaths once and for all. Three months later, however, she realized that she had been dreadfully wrong.

Tonight was Oona's second visit to the park since the accident, and unfortunately for her, she had no dance and no boy to distract her from her thoughts.

Images of the tragedy buzzed in and out of her mind like pestering flies: the sparks shooting from her improvised magic wand, the Lights of Wonder upending the tree and slamming it to the ground, her own panicked cry as the impact hurtled her through the air while Mother and Flora were crushed beneath the tree's massive trunk.

She did her best to shoo the thoughts away, concentrating instead on the contest that was about to begin—the famous Magician's Tower Contest that took place once every five years—but even Oona's excitement about the upcoming competition failed to ease her heart completely. She shook her head, casting around for something solid to hold her attention.

Give me facts! she thought, and pulled her focus to her surroundings.

The tables were set with the finest of crystal and china, the food and drink of the highest caliber. Oona had been to high-society gatherings before—her uncle was extremely fond of parties—but she had not seen so many of the street's wealthy residents in one place since the night of the masquerade three months ago.

She fidgeted with the sleeve of her dress, a high-collared gray-and-white gown, more formal than she was used to wearing. The dress was by no means as extravagant as the dresses worn by the girls from the Academy of Fine Young Ladies, nor was her jewelry as stylish or shiny, but Oona had an idea that it was more than her attire that caused the party guests to glance discreetly in her direction. Oona was something of a celebrity on the street, after all: the youngest Wizard's apprentice in over a hundred years, and it was no secret that she was a Natural Magician: the rarest and most powerful form of magician there was.

As Oona had discovered for herself, it was because of the ancient faerie blood that ran through her veins that her own magic was so incredibly powerful. The deaths of her mother and sister were common knowledge, and rumors of her ability to perform extraordinary magical tasks—most of which were simply untrue—traveled up and down the street like leaves blown from doorstep to doorstep.

The latest rumor Oona had heard was that she had turned her uncle into a toad when he had told her to brush her teeth. Simply absurd.

First of all, she thought, *Uncle Alexander has never needed to remind me to brush my teeth, because brushing one's teeth is simply the logical way of keeping them from rotting out of one's head.* Thus, it followed that Oona needed no reminders. *And secondly*, she thought, *Uncle Alexander may have indeed been turned into a toad, but that was nearly three months ago, and it was not my doing!*

This was also true. It had been her uncle's lawyer, Mr. Ravensmith—in cahoots with Dark Street's most notorious criminal mastermind, Red Martin—who had done the abhorrent deed.

And thirdly, she thought, *I never use magic if I can help it.* Despite her recent return to the position of Wizard's apprentice, the truth was that, in Oona's opinion, magic remained highly unpredictable.

And if all of this wasn't enough to justify the uncomfortable stares, then there was the fact that Oona was the only person with a raven on her shoulder—and a talking raven at that. But of this, Oona did not care what people thought. Deacon was not only Oona's closest companion, but also a wealth of facts and highly useful information.

"Welcome, welcome, welcome!" cried the man on the stage. The chatter of the party guests tapered off, and all eyes turned to observe the squat man at the front of the stage. He wore a tight fitting suit and a top hat nearly as tall as he was. His small eyes took in the well-to-do onlookers. "Welcome to the Magician's Tower. I am Nathaniel Tempest, the tower architect."

A round of applause began. Oona did not join in.

"I don't know if I'd be so proud of that," she whispered to Deacon.

The tower swayed precariously in the breeze, giving the impression it might topple at any moment. The middle portion leaned south, rising slantwise for nearly thirty feet before overcorrecting and tilting north. A set of rickety steps corkscrewed around the outside, and near the seventh floor the entire structure bulged out like a great serpent swallowing an egg. The sound of creaking wood could be heard from as far away as the Iron Gates.

"Look at that monstrosity of a building," Oona half whispered.

Deacon stifled a laugh as the Wizard gave her a disapproving glance from his seat beside her. Dressed in his traditional hood and robe, the Wizard made an imposing figure, as was befitting the head of all magical activity on Dark Street. Oona considered him for a moment. Despite the fact that the only living magicians on the street were the Wizard himself and Oona, the position was still highly respected in the community, and one day, Oona knew, it would belong to her.

"Once every five years," the man in the top hat

continued, "a new tower is constructed, and a new contest begun. It is a contest that stretches back hundreds of years. Anyone brave enough to enter"—the man paused to gesture toward a slanted door at the base of the tower— "will have a chance at solving the first day's challenges . . . but only the first four contestants to make it through the trials will move on to the second day's challenge. After that, two more challenges a day will be offered: a test of the mind and a test of the physical kind. Each day the last contestant to finish will be eliminated, until there are only two left. On the fourth and last day of the contest, both finalists will have an opportunity to solve the final challenge, at the tower's pinnacle; a task so difficult that, in its entire history, it has never been accomplished."

The crowd was silent. Heads tilted back, and all eyes stared up at the pyramid at the very top of the tower. It swayed dauntingly in the night air, barely visible against the night sky. It reminded Oona of the Goblin Tower in the Dark Street Cemetery, at the top of which she had rescued her uncle from imprisonment, except that the Magician's Tower in front of her appeared as if it might crumble at any moment, and the Goblin Tower had stood for nearly five hundred years.

"The contest begins tomorrow at noon!" the man cried. "I am the only one who knows its secrets, and the challenges that lay inside." He held up a leather satchel.

"Only I hold the plans and the answers to the puzzles that await those brave few."

Again a round of applause filled the park, and this time Oona clapped along. Indeed, of everyone at the gathering, it was Oona who clapped the most enthusiastically. Here at last was a challenge she could embrace. As much as she disliked admitting it, her new detective business had been rather slow to catch on. She'd had only two cases in the last three months, one of them involving a missing nail file, and the other, a six-year-old girl who had hired Oona to discover the truth surrounding the existence of something called the Easter Bunny. It was most embarrassing.

But now, finally, here was a worthy challenge. The famous Magician's Tower Contest.

"Please enjoy the rest of the party," the architect said over the applause before descending the stage steps and mingling with the partygoers.

The Wizard turned to Oona. "I take it that you plan to participate in this fiasco."

"I do indeed, Uncle," Oona said. "Not only participate, but win."

"And what is the point?" Deacon asked from her shoulder.

Oona shook her head. "The point, my dearest Deacon, is to be the first. To solve the game. To overcome the mystery. What further point is needed?"

"Well, I suppose I can relieve you of your apprentice duties for the four days of the contest," the Wizard said. "I can get Samuligan to cover for you."

Oona grinned appreciatively. Samuligan, the Pendulum House faerie servant, would be more than equal to the task.

The Wizard glanced in the direction of the table closest to their own, his face sticking out of his hood and exposing a bumpy nose and long gray beard. Oona turned as well, drawn in by a loud voice at the neighboring table. The voice was that of Sir Baltimore Rutherford, one of the most well-known men of Dark Street high society. A handsome man in his mid-fifties, with thick sideburns and a prominent brow, Sir Baltimore waved a pungent cigar in the air, and was laughing heartily at his own joke. The occupants at his table were riveted.

"As I was saying," Sir Baltimore boomed, "when I was a boy, a few years older than my son Roderick is—where is Roderick, anyway? Probably off with that new girlfriend of his. That boy's got more girls pining for him than I'd care to count. But when I was about his age, I, too, participated in the tower contest, and I made it to the top. There were just two of us left: myself and Bradford Crate."

Oona's heart lurched at the mention of her father. She of course knew that her father—the former head inspector of the Dark Street Police Department—had participated in the tower contest, but she had not learned this fact from the man himself. Or if she had, then she had been too young to remember. The fact remained that her full knowledge of her father's youthful adventures in the contest had come from research in books. The thought saddened her. Indeed, there was so much about her father that she did not know, and would most likely never know; the bullet fired from the barrel of a thief's gun had made sure of that nearly three years ago. The loss of her father, only months before losing her mother and sister, had been like a terrible earthquake, shaking Oona's world down to its foundations. "Bradford was the more clever of the two of us," Sir Baltimore continued, "but I had the advantage of my fantastic memory. Runs in the family, you know. I can remember every joke anyone has ever told me."

"Oh, that is wonderful. I wish I could remember jokes," said a sulky-looking woman at Sir Baltimore's table. "But, alas, the moment I hear one, it's in one ear and out the other."

"Well, as I said, it's a family trait," Sir Baltimore said, and then turned abruptly in his seat. "Speaking of inheriting family traits, if it isn't young Miss Crate herself." His smile was a pleasant one. "I was just recalling the time when your father and I went head to head in the tower contest. I was fifteen, and he, I believe, was a few years older. The challenge on the third day was a kind of maze where—"

"Daddy!" cried a voice, cutting Sir Baltimore short. The voice was high and shrill.

"Yes, dear?" Sir Baltimore said, turning to the young girl seated beside him. She looked to be no more than seven years old, and Oona knew her name was Penelope Rutherford.

"Daddy, read me my story now!" Penelope demanded, and thrust a book out toward her father.

"I'm telling my own story, Penny," Sir Baltimore replied.

"No!" the girl shouted. "I want you to read one from *my* book. My favorite book."

Sir Baltimore sighed. "But don't you want to hear how Daddy used his extraordinary powers of memory to find his way out of the tower maze?"

"No!" Penelope exclaimed. "I want to hear about Boon Boon, the man-eating parakeet!"

Sir Baltimore rolled his eyes before turning back to Oona. "Well, it's no matter. In the end, your father beat me out of the maze. I'll never know how he did it."

"Because my younger brother was as clever as they get," said the Wizard.

Sir Baltimore's eyes narrowed slightly. "Yes, Alexander, Bradford was clever."

"You are not still jealous, are you, Baltimore?" asked the Wizard.

"Certainly not. I fell ill the night before the final challenge, and was unable to think straight. Otherwise, I feel certain I should not have answered the final riddle incorrectly. Bradford got it right, of course, but failed to solve the final physical challenge. He was unable to open the puzzle box, just like every contestant before him. Don't forget that, Alexander." Sir Baltimore stubbed out his cigar on his plate and snatched the book of faerie tales from his daughter's hand. He stood. "Come, Penny. Let's find a more quiet atmosphere in which to read."

The two of them stalked off, though rather than head for the outskirts of the park, Sir Baltimore headed for the cluster of partygoers around the architect's table.

"That was a bit harsh, Uncle," Oona said, surprised at her uncle's accusation that Sir Baltimore had been jealous of her father.

The Wizard smiled. "I suppose it was. But they were rivals back then, Baltimore Rutherford and your father. That was before Baltimore ran off to England and somehow managed to get himself knighted, and became *Sir Baltimore.*"

"According to the *Dark Street Who's Who,*" Deacon interjected, "Sir Baltimore Rutherford won his knighthood in a card game against the Earl of Dudley."

Oona grinned appreciatively at the raven. A present from her uncle on her eleventh birthday, Deacon was an enchanted bird whose vast memory contained not only the entire *Encyclopedia Arcanna* and the complete *Oxford English Dictionary,* but also several other helpful volumes that Oona often needed quick access to in her detective work, including the *Dark Street Who's Who,* a book listing virtually every person ever to have lived on the street.

"Yes," the Wizard replied. "If there is any family trait more prominent than the Rutherford *memory,* then it would be the Rutherford *gambling.*"

"How do you mean?" Oona asked.

Deacon answered in a hushed tone: "It is rumored that Sir Baltimore got himself into so much debt with Red Martin that he was forced to give up ownership of his family home as payment. Quite a humiliation for such an esteemed family. Lady Rutherford, his wife, is so embarrassed that she rarely shows her face in public. The Rutherfords still live in the home, but they now pay rent to Red Martin's Nightshade Corporation."

Oona's teeth clenched at the mention of Red Martin's name. The head of the Dark Street criminal underground was presently in hiding because of his involvement in the attack on the Wizard, and since learning that Red Martin was responsible for her father's death, she would have liked nothing more than to see the scoundrel locked behind bars, along with the despicable Mr. Ravensmith. But Red Martin had failed to show up at the trial, and many believed he was now hiding somewhere on the street, still in control of the criminal element.

But Oona had information that most people did not. She knew that Red Martin had found a way through the Glass Gates—the enormous crystal gateway at the south end of Dark Street, which had been magically locked for over five hundred years—and that he had been smuggling all sorts of magical objects across the Faerie border for hundreds of years. One of those items had been turlock root, a magical tuber that Red Martin rubbed on his skin in order to keep himself from growing old. This, Oona concluded, meant that Red Martin was more than likely hiding in Faerie.

Glancing around the party, Oona's heart gave a little start as she recognized a face in the crowd: the tattooed face of Adler Iree, the very boy she had attended the Dark Street Annual Midnight Masquerade with. Due to the fact that his family spent several months of the year living "off street" in New York City, she hadn't seen Adler since the night of the dance. He sat near the far end of the stage, his handsome face hovering over an open book on the table. She was delighted to see him.

At thirteen, Adler was the youngest law student at the Magicians Legal Alliance, and yet in his short period of learning, his cheeks had already been decorated with the alliance's runelike tattoos, each of which indicated the successful completion of a new course of study. Dressed in his customary shabby cloak and frayed top hat, he did not appear to see her, but her heart rate rose at the sight of him.

"Excuse me, Uncle," Oona said. "I see someone I would like to speak to."

Beneath the canopy of lantern-strung trees, she made her way across the park, growing more and more nervous. It had been three months since she had last seen Adler. Would he still want to talk to her, or would he have forgotten her altogether? She certainly hadn't forgotten him. She could remember the serious look on his face as the tattoos crinkled about his eyes in concentration during the waltz. She could also remember the sting of his feet stepping on her toes several times, though it was not an unpleasant thought, and, admittedly, the toe stepping had been just as much her fault as it had been his.

Presently, most of the partygoers were on their feet, and Oona slipped around the empty tables, squeezing nimbly through a sea of tuxedo tails and bustled dresses. She was playing a little game with herself as she moved, trying not to touch anyone as she bobbed and weaved her way across the park, when she suddenly found herself nearly knocked off her feet. She stumbled back in surprise, looking hurriedly around, only to discover that she had collided with what appeared to be a moving pile of rags. Deacon cawed noisily from her shoulder at the unexpected jostle.

"A thousand pardons," said the pile of rags, and Oona's heart leapt, more from the unexpected voice coming from the rags than from being so violently jostled. And then she realized that this was not just a pile of rags, but a woman draped from head to foot in jaggedly cut cloth. The woman looked wildly out of place among the well-dressed party guests.

"Please, do be forgiving me," said the woman, her voice old and cracked, like ancient wallpaper. The heavy smell of mint did little to disguise the reek of her breath, and Oona stepped back to avoid the pungent odor. The woman continued to speak in a thick, foreign-sounding accent: "I am Madame Romania from Romania, and I am here to be telling the fortunes of these fine guests."

"Oh, a fortune-teller," Oona said, unable to keep the skepticism from her voice.

"Would you like your fortune told, young miss?" asked Madame Romania from Romania. "My caravan is parked just over there, and I can be giving you the answers to very many of the questions."

Oona shook her head, thinking to herself that, if any question truly needed to be answered, it would be how to cure such terrible breath.

"No, thank you," Oona said. "I'm looking for some-one, but thank you for—"

The woman's hand shot out quick as a snake, grab-bing Oona's wrist and squeezing tight. Oona took in a startled breath, suddenly frightened.

"You are not responsible for the burden you hold!" Madame Romania from Romania said in an urgent, hushed tone.

"Release her at once!" Deacon demanded, poising himself on Oona's shoulder, ready to attack.

But at the sound of the woman's words, Oona froze. She blinked in surprise, staring into the woman's eyes, which were the only part of the fortune-teller she could see. And then Madame Romania from Romania released her grip, pulling her hand back so that it disappeared within the tangle of multicolored fabrics.

"Please do be forgiving me," she said. "I do not mean to be frightening the young miss. But Madame Romania from Romania sees."

Oona rubbed at her wrist, looking wary. "What do you mean I am not responsible for the burden I hold?" But Oona thought she knew exactly what the gypsy was speaking of. The laughing faces of her mother and baby sister filled her head.

The gypsy woman shrugged. "Madame Romania from Romania is not so sure what she means. We would need to be consulting the punchbowl to see these things clearly."

"The punchbowl?" Oona asked quizzically.

"Yes," the woman said, and she stepped closer to Oona. "The Punchbowl Oracle can show you all the answers you seek." She pointed toward a wagon—her large, box-like gypsy caravan—which was parked near the far end of the stage. Small bells hung from the caravan's windows and tinkled in the breeze. "I am having the bowl there, inside for the safekeeping. You may visit if you are liking to know much answers."

The woman abruptly spun on her heels and trotted away in the direction of the caravan.

Oona hesitated, and as she stared after the fortune-teller, she felt a tap on her shoulder. She turned to discover Isadora Iree—Adler Iree's twin sister—standing behind her in the ghostly lamplight. A gorgeous girl only a few months older than Oona, Isadora grinned, her enormous blue eyes blinking prettily in the flickering glow from above. Beside Isadora stood the most handsome boy Oona had ever seen. With short, well-groomed blond hair, high cheekbones, and a square-shaped chin, the two of them—Isadora and the boy—made quite a picture.

"Oona, darling," said Isadora, as if the two of them were the best of friends, "it is good to see you."

Isadora wore a pretty blue-and-white patterned dress,

with an extravagant pink shawl. Why Isadora was being so nice to her, Oona couldn't have said. The two of them had never gotten along well, and Isadora's pleasantness put Oona on her guard.

"Hello, Isadora," Oona said warily. "You are looking lovely."

Isadora's eyes flicked quickly over Oona's appearance, but she did not return the compliment. She held her hand out toward the well-dressed boy.

"This is my BOYFRIEND," she said so forcefully that Oona nearly stepped back.

The boy smiled at Oona, displaying a set of marvelously straight teeth. "Roderick Rutherford," he said, and extended his hand.

A look crossed Isadora's face as if she might swat Roderick's hand back, but she somehow managed to control herself. Oona took Roderick's hand and shook.

"The son of Sir Baltimore," Deacon intoned from Oona's shoulder.

"Indeed," said Roderick.

"And did I mention that he's my BOYFRIEND?" Isadora asked.

Oona worked hard to suppress a smile. "I believe you did, Isadora. And a fine couple you do make."

What followed was a long, awkward moment in which Isadora and Roderick appeared to strike a pose. Oona spotted a splotch of mud on the shoulder of Roderick's well-fitted jacket. She squinted, as if not seeing correctly, and then realized that one entire sleeve of his jacket was dripping wet. Roderick followed her gaze to the spot on his shoulder, but did not seem surprised to see the mud there.

"Oh, this," he said, then gestured vaguely in the direction of the gypsy caravan. "Isadora was about to step in a puddle. It's very muddy."

Oona shook her head. "But how did the mud get on your shoulder?"

"My BOYFRIEND didn't want me to have to walk around," said Isadora. "So my BOYFRIEND put his jacket down over the puddle, so that I wouldn't muddy the bottom of my dress." She squeezed Roderick's arm tightly, looking like a child who's received an expensive new toy. "Isn't my BOYFRIEND wonderful?"

"Chivalry!" said Roderick, as if announcing the answer to some unasked question. "It is all about chivalry. Like the knights of King Arthur. No deed is too small, no task too large for my lady. She need only ask, and I'll scale the city walls, battle a sea monster, slay a dragon, or bake cookies. I am a modern chivalrous."

Deacon shuddered. "A person cannot be a chivalrous! It is an adjective. The proper term would be a chevalier."

Roderick seemed not to have heard. "Chivalry!

Chivalry! Chivalry!" he intoned, and then fell silent, reveling in himself.

For a long moment Oona did not know how to respond. Finally, she pointed toward the back of a woman standing nearby. The woman's dress flowed outward in extravagant lavenders and blues.

"Isn't that your mother, Isadora?" Oona asked. "I do believe I saw that dress in her shop window only last week."

The corners of Isadora's mouth turned downward. "That is not my mother, nor is it my mother's dress. It is a copy . . . a knockoff."

Isadora spun around, pointing in the direction of the crowd near the stage. There, beside the architect, stood the real Madame Iree, a matronly woman with a prodigious bosom who just happened to be the most exclusive dressmaker on all of Dark Street. The dress Madame Iree wore appeared identical to the one worn by the lady standing nearby.

Oona was just about to excuse herself from Isadora and Roderick's company, intent on tracking down Madame Romania from Romania, when a commotion broke out near the architect's table.

"My dress!" Madame Iree shouted. "You've spilled your soup all over it!"

Oona could just make out the figures of the architect

and Madame Iree lying in a heap on the ground. The stunned-looking architect was attempting to push himself up with one hand while holding an empty bowl in his other.

"I'm so sorry, madame. Please excuse my clumsiness," said the architect as several hands from the crowd reached out to help them both back to their feet.

"Don't be ridiculous!" said an enormous man standing nearby. Oona recognized him to be Mr. Bop, the tattoo-faced senior undersecretary from the Magicians Legal Alliance. "I saw the whole thing, and *she* is the one who bumped into *you*."

The architect appeared confused. "Well . . . I don't know what happened, but do please accept my apologies, madame."

"Now I shall have to return home for a change of wardrobe!" Madame Iree announced before making a rather dramatic exit across the park.

"Poor Mother," said Isadora. "Can you think of anything more dreadful than having soup spilled on your dress?"

"I can think of countless things that are far worse than—" Deacon began, but Oona cut him short.

"It was lovely speaking to you, Isadora," Oona lied. "And a pleasure to meet you, Mr. Rutherford. Please excuse me."

"The pleasure was mine," Roderick replied.

Oona turned away just as Isadora's mouth wrinkled into a frown. "Don't forget you're *my BOYFRIEND*."

"Of course, Isadora, my lady. I was only saying . . . ," but Roderick's voice trailed off as Oona and Deacon pressed through the crowd, her original interest in finding Adler Iree all at once squashed by the urge to learn more of what the gypsy had to say.

The caravan was a large box-type wagon, festooned with ornate molding and draping swaths of shiny cloth. A sign painted in large black letters across the side exclaimed:

MADAME ROMANIA FROM ROMANIA! FORTUNES TOLD, PALMS READ, SECRETS REVEALED INSIDE!

"You aren't seriously considering talking to that fortune-teller, are you?" Deacon asked.

Oona's face flushed red, and she paused on the step leading up to the caravan door.

"She'll simply take your money and tell you some bit of vague nonsense," Deacon added.

"I . . . yes, I suppose you're right," Oona said, not wishing to explain how the gypsy's words had sparked a flame of hope in her that she had thought long dead. "But it could be fun."

Oona moved to the second step. One of the flyers announcing the opening of the tower contest had been tacked to the door. It read:

TAKE THE ULTIMATE CHALLENGE.

BE THE ULTIMATE HERO.

IT'S THE MAGICIAN'S TOWER CONTEST.

TOUR THE DEPTHS OF THE MIND.

OVERCOME PHYSICAL TASKS AT RISK OF LIFE AND LIMB.

MUST BE AT LEAST THIRTEEN YEARS OLD TO ENTER THE TOWER.

WINNER RECEIVES A PLAQUE AT THE MUSEUM

(COURTESY OF MCMILLAN'S TROPHY SHOP)

AND WILL GO DOWN IN MAGICAL HISTORY.

Oona reached for the doorknob. Her hand froze. A sudden shout pulled her attention in the direction of the stage.

It was the architect.

"The plans!" he shouted. "The plans for the tower contest are missing from my satchel. Someone call the police!"

Oona's pulse quickened, and a smile creased the corners of her mouth.

"A case," she whispered.

"A case, indeed," Deacon said excitedly.

And then Oona was running toward the commotion, Deacon soaring just above her head like a shadowy thought. By the time she forced her way through the crowd, her heart was pounding.

"What has happened?" she asked.

"Who are you?" asked the architect. The squat little man looked as white as a ghost.

"I am Oona Crate. I heard you say that the plans had been stolen."

The crowd muttered in hushed tones all around them.

"Yes, yes," said the architect. He patted his satchel. "The plans were in here. All of the tower's secrets. They must be found, or the contest will have to be cancelled."

Oona peered around at the crowd, wondering if whoever had stolen the plans might still be among them. There were many familiar faces: Mr. Bop, Isadora Iree, and Roderick Rutherford were clustered near Oona's uncle. Adler Iree stood from his table, his top hat askew, the arcane tattoos on his face scrunched up in an expression of concern. The woman wearing the knockoff version of Madame Iree's dress held her gloved hand to her forehead, as if she might swoon. Sir Baltimore and Mr. Glump, the curator from the Museum of Magical History, were there to steady her.

As she took in the faces of possible suspects, Oona was taken completely by surprise when Deacon announced: "Here they are!"

"Here are what?" Oona asked, spinning round to discover Deacon standing on the ground near the edge of the crowd. He was poking his beak at several pieces of parchment.

The crowd stepped away to reveal the pages.

"The plans," Deacon said.

"But . . . why are they there on the ground?" Oona asked.

"That is obviously where you dropped them!" said a high, knifelike voice. Oona closed her eyes and shook her head. She knew that voice. Knew it all too well. She spun around to discover Inspector White of the Dark Street Police Department stepping through the crowd. He stooped to retrieve the papers.

"Clearly," the inspector continued, "it was you, Miss Crate, who stole the plans, so that you would have the advantage in the contest."

"Don't be ridiculous," said Deacon as he flew to Oona's shoulder. "She was nowhere near the architect, or his satchel."

Oona thrust her hands to her hips. "And besides," she said, all at once concerned with her eligibility for the contest, "I wouldn't have had time to read them."

"A likely story," said the inspector.

"Perhaps the plans simply fell out by accident," said the architect.

Oona looked at the architect's leather satchel, with its thick strap and heavy brass buckle, and thought it highly unlikely that this could have been the case.

Inspector White knelt down to get a closer look at the satchel. He examined it one handed, still holding the recovered plans in his other hand.

"I believe you are right," he said at last, and then handed the plans back to the architect. "The plans obviously fell out of the satchel on their own." He straightened. "It seems you are off the hook this time, Miss Crate. But be warned. I'll be keeping a close watch on this contest. And any shady activity will get you disqualified . . . not to mention thrown into the police dungeon."

Oona was taken aback. She was used to Inspector White's accusations that she was up to no good, or had committed this crime or that, but the threat of disqualification from the contest seemed to hit home. Rather than argue with the incompetent man, she decided to let the matter of the tower plans go. So what if it was nearly impossible for the plans to have fallen out of the satchel on their own? What did it matter, really? They had been found with no harm done.

"Well, thank goodness you showed up," Oona said to the inspector. "Who knows what sort of chaos this might have turned into."

The inspector jabbed his pale thumbs into his waistband, looking very pleased with himself.

Oona made her way slowly back across the park. She felt a touch of disappointment at the false alarm. It would have been nice to have had a real case.

Deacon seemed to read her thoughts. "Perhaps it's best that there was no case. The tower contest will require your full attention."

"No doubt you're right," she said. "Yet you know those plans did not fall out on their own."

Deacon nodded thoughtfully. "True, but they were found."

"Yes. That was an excellent observation on your part, Deacon."

"Do not mention it."

Looking up, Oona found herself once again in front of the gypsy caravan. She noticed how the letters on the side of the wagon appeared freshly painted, and even thought she could smell the paint.

"Look," said Deacon, "Madame Iree returns."

Isadora's mother, Madame Iree, could be seen making her way back across the park to the party, now dressed in a magnificent new dress, this one emerald green with white lace, and a bustle at the back so large it resembled a camel's hump.

"That was a quick change," Oona said.

Deacon shrugged. "You are still planning on engaging with this fortune-teller?"

Oona considered the door to the caravan, but shook her head. Deacon was correct. It was ridiculous to consult with such a woman, but just as she was about to turn and go, the door at the back of the wagon opened and Madame Romania from Romania put out her hand.

"Ah, yes. I was knowing you would come. Yes. I have the sight, I do, as did my mother, and her mother, and all the mothers going back in much, much history."

Deacon shivered at the terrible English, but kept his beak closed.

"Do be coming in, please. Yes, yes." The fortune-teller beckoned with one rag-covered finger.

The smell of sage and incense wafted through the door, and the bells along the outside of the wagon tinkled. Oona felt torn. Her curiosity was brimming, yet she also felt that Deacon was correct to warn against dealing with such a dubious character. In the end, however, the urge to hear what the woman had to say was too strong to resist. She took in a deep breath and followed the old woman inside.

A curtain of beads clattered as Oona stepped into a

smoky room. Thick, velvety fabrics of black, purple, and gold hung from the walls. Silver charms and bundles of sticks tied together with string dangled from the ceiling. A low, round table stood at the center of the space, with fat cushions on either side. Madame Romania from Romania disappeared through a slit in a red velvet curtain, and Oona could hear her moving around behind it.

"Please, do be taking the seat at the table," the gypsy called. "I am getting bowl. You may ask one question, and it will be giving you true answer."

Oona was reluctant to take a seat, feeling nervous, and not quite understanding why. She swallowed back her nerves and hesitantly lowered herself onto one of the cushioned seats, suffering through the doubt that she should be here at all.

The old woman continued moving around behind the curtain that divided the front half of the caravan from the back. A moment later she reappeared through the slit with a large, plain-looking wooden box in her hands.

"This is where bowl sleeps," she said. "It must to be sleeping at least the five minutes before each question."

"Ah, I see," Oona said quite untruthfully.

Madame Romania from Romania set the box on the table and began fumbling with the latch.

"Latch is stubborn. It is sticking. I must to be getting it fixed. And . . . ah, there we go. Now we will see what bowl has to say about—" But Madame Romania from Romania took in a startled breath, and then let loose a shriek so loud that it caused all the tiny hairs along Oona's arms to stick straight up.

Deacon leapt into the air as Oona jumped to her feet. "Madame Romania, what is it?" she asked.

The gypsy woman opened the box fully, her eyes wide. Her hands shook, and her mouth hung open, expelling her noxious, mint-tinged breath directly into Oona's face. Madame Romania from Romania stood that way for what might have been ten long seconds before finally taking in a sob-filled breath and exclaiming: "The Punchbowl Oracle! It is gone! It has been stolen!"

CHAPTER TWO

Breakfast at Pendulum House

The dining hall was the longest room in Pendulum House. It stretched nearly a hundred feet from the room's entrance to the servant's door on the other side. The wall to the left displayed a mural depicting a dramatic scene of Oswald the Great, his wand in hand, scarlet light streaming from its tip as he aimed it at the enormous Glass Gates.

Oona sat at the farthest end of the long table, staring absently at her breakfast. Her uncle sat at the head of the table, reading the morning edition of *The Dark Street Tribune*. Its bold headline read: "Tower Contest Begins Today." Beneath the fold of the paper, a smaller headline read: "Enchanted Objects Continue to Plague Street."

The Wizard shook his head. "According to this article, there have been two cases of pixiewood poisoning this week. Horrible stuff. Turns the skin green for weeks, and in some cases the victims start to sprout branches like a tree. What the paper doesn't know, however, is that there have actually been four total cases that I have dealt with in the past month. And at least I have a cure for the poison, but it seems there have also been reports of throttler's silk turning up in the garment district. It's a faerie silk known to slowly strangle its wearer." The Wizard shuddered. "The thing is, all of these objects come from only one place: Faerie. Certainly no Wizard ever made such abhorrent things. Nevertheless, they're giving my enchantment shop a bad name. People are becoming more and more afraid of magic. No doubt I will be called out to deal with the silk. It will need to be destroyed."

The Wizard glanced around the table, but no one seemed to be paying the slightest attention.

Deacon was perched on the arm of a candelabrum, while Samuligan stood at the corner of the table, perfectly still and thin as a whip. Bewitched into a lifetime of service nearly five hundred years ago—and as far as Oona knew, the only living faerie this side of the Glass Gates—Samuligan stood six and a half feet tall, his smart butler's attire hanging from bony shoulders. Pointed ears and a hooked nose gave the faerie an unmistakably nonhuman air, yet it was his brilliant eyes that proved to be his most striking feature. They were haunting, mischievous eyes that often remained hidden beneath the shadowy brim of his cowboy hat.

"Have the witches received their ration of turlock root this month, Samuligan?" the Wizard asked.

"They have," replied the faerie servant in his sly, hushed voice. "I delivered it to the police dungeons last week. They remain as young as ever."

The Wizard nodded. "Their time served for the theft of the magical mind daggers is almost up, is it not?"

"Two more weeks of imprisonment," Deacon replied. "Then they may return to Witch Hill. It is a short amount of time when you consider that the girls are over five hundred years old. Will you continue to provide them with turlock root once they have been released?"

"I gave my word that I would," the Wizard said. "It was the witches' testimony that convinced the jury that Red Martin was involved in my attack. For that I agreed to provide them with enough root to keep them alive . . . though perhaps we will limit their consumption, so that they will age normally, like everyone else."

"Everyone?" Samuligan asked.

The Wizard looked up at the faerie servant and chuckled. "Well, like every human, anyway. Immortality does not suit us human beings like it does you faeries, Samuligan. What do you think, Oona?"

Oona, who was inattentively picking at the crumbly muffin on her plate, looked up. "I'm sorry, Uncle. What did you say?"

The Wizard frowned. "You have barely touched your breakfast, Oona." He folded his paper and placed it on the table. "You should eat something. You'll need the energy."

"I'm . . . not so hungry," Oona said.

"Well, maybe you'd like something else," he turned to the faerie servant. "Perhaps she would prefer a meat pie, Samuligan."

Samuligan nodded. "Of course, sir," he said, and a smile appeared on his face like a sickly crescent moon. Before Oona could protest, a guttural sound emanated from the back of Samuligan's throat. The muffin all at once disappeared from her plate, only to be replaced with a large, thick-crusted pie, steam seeping from the slits in its top.

"That was unnecessary," Oona said, feeling the tingle of goose bumps on her arms from having been so close to the faerie servant's magic. "As I said, I'm simply not hungry."

The Wizard sniffed at the pie before shrugging and sliding the plate over in front of himself. "You aren't still obsessing about that gypsy woman you told me about last night, are you?" he asked, jabbing in his fork and taking a bite. Steam erupted from the pie, momentarily obscuring his face.

Samuligan snapped his fingers and the steam took on the semblance of an enormous toadlike mask. Oona raised an eyebrow at him, not finding the joke as funny as the faerie had intended it to be. She knew he was only trying to cheer her up in his strange fashion, but at the moment Oona was too preoccupied with the memory of the curious events of the previous night to be entertained by the magic.

Samuligan on the other hand seemed quite amused with himself. The faerie threw back his head and barked with laughter, causing the Wizard's teacup to explode and startling Deacon into the air.

"Oh, now, Samuligan, look what you've done," said the Wizard, who had been drenched with tea and dribbled some of his pie down his beard.

True to form, Samuligan reached into his pocket and pulled out an entire mop, which he proceeded to use to clean up the spillage.

"Is that what you are brooding about?" the Wizard asked Oona as Samuligan dabbed at his beard with the mop head. The Wizard swatted it away. "That business with the missing crystal ball?"

"It wasn't a crystal ball," Oona said irritably. "It was called the Punchbowl Oracle."

"She's been up nearly all night, obsessing over its disappearance," Deacon said, landing back on the candelabrum.

Oona shot him a reproachful glance. It was true, she had been up most of the night attempting to piece together some picture of what had happened, but the last thing she wanted was to explain to her uncle precisely *why* she was so concerned about the punchbowl's disappearance—namely, Madame Romania from Romania's claim that she, Oona, was not responsible for some burden. A secret that only the Punchbowl Oracle had the power to reveal.

If there was a chance—even the faintest glimmer of a possibility—that Oona had not been responsible for her mother's and sister's deaths, then she absolutely had to find out, and that meant that she needed to discover what had happened to the bowl.

Her uncle, like Deacon, would no doubt tell Oona that such fortune-tellers were nothing but frauds who told a person exactly what he or she wanted to hear in order to make easy money.

But Madame Romania from Romania had asked for no money, and after the punchbowl's disappearance, Oona had listened intently as the woman explained how going to the police was out of the question.

"Gypsies are not to be getting very much along with the police," Madame Romania from Romania had assured

Oona, before noisily blowing her nose into her ragged sleeve and falling into a sobbing fit of grief.

This in mind, Oona reasoned that if she did not solve the mystery, then no one else would. And while it was true that the gypsy woman had not specifically asked for Oona's help, she had not asked her *not* to help either. And the truth of it was, if Madame Romania from Romania was correct, then the Punchbowl Oracle—a crystal bowl precisely seven inches deep and thirteen inches in diameter—was the only fortune-telling device capable of not only showing the future, but also showing the past. It could answer any question, and indeed held the power to show Oona exactly what had happened the day of her mother's death.

One pestering bit of information continued to needle at Oona's thoughts: Madame Romania from Romania's insistence that the door to the caravan had been locked tight while she was away. No one could have gotten in. And yet with the punchbowl missing, Oona believed this impossible. She yearned to have a good look around the wagon for some clue—a sign of forced entry, or perhaps a loose floorboard—but in her grief over the missing punchbowl, the ragged gypsy woman had given Oona very few details before hurrying her out the caravan door and locking herself inside.

Today, during daylight, Oona thought, *would be the perfect time to investigate, and yet . . .*

As if reading her thoughts, the Wizard said: "You should put the punchbowl out of your mind, Oona. Concentrate your efforts on the contest."

Put a mystery out of her mind? Before it was solved? *Ridiculous*, she thought. She had a good mind to tell her uncle just that, but instead she simply nodded, and said: "Yes, Uncle. I'll do my best."

The response seemed to satisfy the Wizard, who rammed another piping-hot glob of pie into his mouth. Deacon, who knew better than to trust a response like that from Oona, tutted, and Oona threw him a warning glance. But Deacon couldn't seem to help himself.

"According to the *Encyclopedia Arcanna*," he recited, "fortune-telling is a capricious art at best—meaning that predicting the future is . . . well . . . unpredictable." Deacon paused, as if waiting for a laugh. When none came, he cleared his throat. "There is no mention of a Punchbowl Oracle in the encyclopedia whatsoever, nor any object with such prophetic powers. None in this world, that is."

"An Orb of Cathesis could do as much," Samuligan interjected.

"Yes, Samuligan," said the Wizard. "But Orbs of Cathesis existed only in Faerie."

Deacon fluttered to Oona's shoulder. "There is no record of an orb ever having crossed from one world to the other. Even if one had, the orbs, of which there were only ten, were created to answer only one question each. They would most likely have all been used up by now."

"Will it be difficult?" Oona asked in order to change the subject. "The contest, I mean. The Magician's Tower Contest."

As the Wizard had just taken another bite of pie, it was Samuligan who answered. "The Magician's Tower Contest has been taking place for nearly as long as I have been serving the occupants of Pendulum House. It takes place every five years, and I have seen nearly one hundred of them. They are always amusing to watch . . ." The mop Samuligan was holding all at once turned into a sword, which he pointed at Deacon: "And often deadly."

Deacon made a loud squawk, hopping from his perch on the candelabrum to the table.

"It is true," said the Wizard. "People have died, in the past, but only because they were foolhardy and did not take the challenges seriously."

Samuligan shrugged, as if death were nothing to fear. His sword changed into a trumpet, which he blew forcefully into the air before adding: "But mostly the applicants suffer only superficial wounds."

Oona knew all of this, of course. She had been preparing for the contest for the past month, researching previous challenges with Deacon.

"Is it true that the challenges are never the same from one competition to the next?" she asked.

"They are always new," the Wizard said.

"Except for the final challenge," Samuligan put in. "It is always the same . . . and has never been completed."

"The puzzle box," Oona said.

Both Samuligan and the Wizard nodded thoughtfully. The unopenable box, a legendary object that defied solving. It was a mystery that she should dearly love to get her hands on.

"But to get to the final task, you must complete the first three," the Wizard mused. "And that will be difficult to do on an empty stomach."

Oona's stomach grumbled. The thought of the first set of challenges sent a wave of excitement through her. Just then, a memory came to her, one that she couldn't believe she could have ever forgotten. It was a fantastic memory, a fuzzy image of holding her father's hand in Oswald Park and watching the contestants disappear inside the tower.

"One day I'll go in there, and I'll win," she had told her father.

Her father had grinned at her, and then said something that she could not remember. Perhaps it was then that he had told her of his own adventures inside the tower. It bothered her that she could have forgotten that such a moment had existed. She wished that she could remember everything about her parents, but the more time went on, the more she seemed to lose them. Her mother had been there as well, standing beside her father on the grassy ground. She, too, had grinned at Oona and said . . . what? Something like . . .

And then Oona's breath caught in her throat as she remembered the words.

"Of course you will win, darling," her mother had said. "I have the utmost confidence."

And now here Oona was, five years later, getting ready to enter the contest. She wished that her parents could be there to see it. She wanted so badly to make them proud.

"On second thought," she said, turning to Samuligan, "Uncle Alexander is right. Breakfast is exactly what I need. Pancakes please, Samuligan. With lots of butter, and strawberries!"

CHAPTER THREE

The First Clue

O ona was astounded. It appeared that nearly all of Dark Street had turned out to either participate in or watch the contest. From the enormous fountain in the shape of Oswald the Great at the gate entrance, to the soaring red brick wall at the far end, Oswald Park was jam-packed with people of all shapes and sizes. On the other side of that brick wall, Oona knew, was nothing at all—a vast emptiness known as the Drift, where Dark Street swung around and around like an enormous clock hand, coming to rest only once a day, at exactly midnight, when the Iron Gates at the north end of the street opened for one minute upon New York City before closing again and moving on.

Nearly thirteen miles long, Dark Street was home to thousands. Considering that the contest took place only once every five years, it should have been no surprise to Oona that so many people had shown up, yet she could scarcely remember having seen so many of the street's citizens in one place at one time.

It took her longer than she would have liked to make her way to the front of the stage at the base of the crooked tower.

If she had thought that the daylight might have added a tinge of beauty to the monstrosity of a building, she was sorely mistaken. Every rickety curve, kink, and wobbly defect revealed itself in the bright light of day. Oona was forced to crane her neck to see the mysterious pyramid at the top of the tower, where it rocked precariously against the purplish-blue sky. Her stomach turned at the thought of going up there.

With Deacon resting on her shoulder, Oona had only just reached the front of the stage, having forced her way between two overly dressed women, when a high-pitched girly voice grated in Oona's ears.

"Read me a story from my storybook, Daddy!" the voice whined, and Oona could feel Deacon's claws tighten on her shoulder at the sound of it.

Sir Baltimore Rutherford leaned casually against the front of the stage, his young daughter Penelope sitting on the edge beside him. With her scarlet hair pulled back in tight pigtails, and her electric-blue dress puffing out around her like a bell, she looked a bit like a large rag doll, one that had been magically brought to life. She waved a storybook in her father's face.

"Not now, Penelope, dear," said Sir Baltimore. "The contest is about to start. We're here to support your brother."

"But I want to hear the story of the evil chipmunks and the wicked farmer!" Penelope chided.

"I told you, Penny," Sir Baltimore said, "we're here to watch Roderick." Then, as if speaking more to himself, he added: "And he'd better win . . . or else . . ."

But Sir Baltimore did not finish his thought out loud, having suddenly noticed Oona. He tipped his hat. "Ah, Miss Crate. See, Penny. Here is Roderick's most dangerous competition . . . that is, if she is at all like her father."

He laughed idly, but Oona detected a note of seriousness to his tone.

"Hello, Sir Baltimore," she said politely.

Roderick appeared quite suddenly at his father's side, with Isadora Iree in hand, the two of them looking striking as usual. And then Oona's heart fumbled in her chest. Adler Iree stepped through the crowd and tipped his hat.

"Sorry I missed you last night, Miss Crate," he said in his thick Irish accent.

Oona nodded, displaying what she hoped was the socially acceptable amount of a smile, though she felt like beaming at him. With his scruffy old top hat resting cock-eyed on his head, he gave Oona a roguish wink. Oona felt a fluttering in her stomach, and her cheeks grew warm.

"Did you meet my BOYFRIEND?" Isadora asked Oona before she could reply to Adler.

Oona suppressed a smile. "I believe you introduced us last night. Are you all participating in the competition?"

"Oh, yes," said Isadora. "Wouldn't miss it for the world. I suppose you are entering as well?"

Oona nodded. "I am."

Isadora stepped closer and crossed her arms. "Of course, you'll have the advantage with all of that magic stuff you know."

Oona peered up at Isadora, who stood several inches taller, despite the fact that Isadora was less than six months older. Oona knew by Isadora's tone that she was getting at something. "What's that supposed to mean?" Oona asked.

"Oh, nothing," said Isadora. She narrowed one eye, inspecting Oona from head to foot. "I'm just saying that, well, if you were forced to play by the same rules as the rest of us, without magic, you probably wouldn't even make it past the first set of challenges."

"Oh, dear, don't fall for that," Deacon whispered in

Oona's ear. "There are no rules against using magic in the contest. Any advantage you have is fair game."

But Oona wasn't listening. She pointed her chin like a spear at Isadora. "Is that a challenge?"

Deacon groaned.

"It is whatever you make of it," Isadora replied.

Oona's face grew warm. She had fallen for a challenge of Isadora's once before, when the insufferable girl had dared Oona to find Madame Iree's missing dresses before the Midnight Masquerade . . . and in the end, Oona had come out the winner. But this was different. Here, Oona had the clear advantage of using magic to overcome whatever obstacles lay within the Magician's Tower. Her magical abilities would come in quite handy . . . but it irritated her to think that Isadora believed Oona needed magic to win. The truth was, Oona nearly always found nonmagical solutions to be preferable to magic anyway, and she quickly decided she would have none of it.

"Fine," she said. "I won't use any magic at all during the contest, and then we shall see who is the better."

Isadora grinned like a fox. "We shall."

Oona felt a lead weight drop into her stomach, realizing too late that she had done exactly what Isadora had wanted.

"Attention!" called a voice. "The contest is about to begin. May I have your attention, please?"

"That was unwise," Deacon whispered in Oona's ear.

"Oh, hush," Oona said, feeling foolish enough as it was.

The architect took to center stage and spoke through an enormous cone that amplified his voice. The crowd hushed. "The first four contestants to make it through both of today's challenges will continue on to tomorrow's challenge," he announced. "Good luck to you all."

Then came a pause in which Oona could feel Deacon's claws grip at her shoulder. The pause turned into an even longer silence, and then a clock tower chimed in the distance, twelve strokes marking the hour.

"The first clue can be found on the flyer announcing the tower contest!" the architect said through the cone. He adjusted the ridiculously tall hat on his head, adding: "That is all."

He set the cone on the stage before plopping down in a chair, where he crossed his legs, unfolded a newspaper, and began to read as if he were sitting idly in his own living room instead of in front of hundreds of eager eyes.

And then there was pandemonium. Like an explosion, the crowd began to force its way toward the park entrance, participants and spectators alike attempting to get to one of the flyers that had been hung all over the street.

There must have been hundreds of flyers, Oona

realized: red-colored pieces of paper, each announcing the opening of the Magician's Tower Contest. She
remembered seeing them plastered all over town, in shop
windows, on lampposts, the closest of which was . . .
where?

She looked around, certain there must have been
some flyers posted in the park itself, but surprisingly,
there were none to be seen.

Of course, she thought, *the architect wouldn't have made
it that easy.*

"Shall I fly off and get you a flyer?" Deacon offered.

Oona opened her mouth, on the verge of telling him
to hop to it, when she suddenly remembered something
that made her arms prickle with excitement.

"The gypsy caravan!" she said.

"I beg your pardon?" said Deacon.

Oona did not answer. She remembered seeing one
of the contest flyers hanging from the gypsy's back door
only the night before. She whirled around. The caravan
was still parked near the far end of the stage, which was
quite convenient, seeing as the sea of slowly moving
people was heading in the opposite direction.

Oona raced toward the caravan. She circled around
the wagon, and there it was: the flyer she had seen the
night before. She tugged it from its tack and hurriedly
read.

TAKE THE ULTIMATE CHALLENGE.

BE THE ULTIMATE HERO.

IT'S THE MAGICIAN'S TOWER CONTEST.

TOUR THE DEPTHS OF THE MIND.

OVERCOME PHYSICAL TASKS AT RISK OF LIFE AND LIMB.

MUST BE AT LEAST THIRTEEN YEARS OLD TO ENTER THE TOWER.

WINNER RECEIVES A PLAQUE AT THE MUSEUM

(COURTESY OF MCMILLAN'S TROPHY SHOP)

AND WILL GO DOWN IN MAGICAL HISTORY.

The rest of the flyer appeared to be nothing more than an artistic sketch of the tower itself.

"Do you see a clue anywhere?" Deacon asked.

"I'm looking for it, Deacon," Oona said irritably. She removed a small magnifying glass from her dress pocket and began moving it steadily along the illustration. The magnifying glass, which was gold plated around the rim, with a well-worn wooden handle, had been her father's very own glass—and, according to Oona's uncle, her father had been the best head inspector the Dark Street Police Department had ever known.

Indeed, the magnifying glass was so special to Oona that she often felt like she was seeing through her father's eyes when she used it to look for clues. Sometimes she got the feeling that he was there beside her, urging her on, forcing her to see what was really in front of her and not just what *appeared* to be there.

Presently, she peered through the glass at the flyer. It took no more than several seconds to find the hidden clue.

"Aha!" She pointed at a set of numbers that had been cleverly disguised along the edge of the illustration of the tower. "Look, Deacon, do you see? The numbers."

Once her eyes made them out, the magnifying glass became unnecessary to read them.

"I do indeed," Deacon said. "But what do they mean?"

Oona stared hard at the numbers. Running down the side of the tower illustration, from top to bottom, they read: 67, 2, 7, 10, 4, 1, 3, 2, 1.

"A strange bunch of numbers," Deacon observed.

"Strange in what way?" Oona asked.

"Well, I see no immediate pattern," he said. "Except for the 'three, two, one' at the end."

"The end, Deacon?" Oona asked. "And why are you assuming that the numbers run from top to bottom?"

"Well, it only seems natural to read them from the top of the page down."

Oona considered this. While what Deacon had said made sense, Oona couldn't help but feel as if there was something a little too obvious about it. It was a feeling she had, an intuition that she should look for some other logical way to read the numbers. A moment later, she had it. She felt a surge of excitement, and more than a pinch of pride at having figured it out so quickly.

"Reading the numbers top to bottom would be natural, yes," she said. "And yet, look where the numbers are, Deacon. What are the numbers supposed to *be* in the illustration?"

Deacon leaned closer, cocking his head to one side. "I don't follow you. They simply look as if they are part of the tower."

Oona nodded. "Yes, Deacon. And it is my experience that the numbers in buildings run from the first floor, at the bottom, and go upward in sequence."

"Ah, I see your point," he said. "The numbers could easily be read from bottom to top. One, two, three, one, four, ten, seven, two, sixty-seven."

Oona stared up at the tower. She saw no indication of numbers anywhere.

"Perhaps they are referring to the different floors of the tower," Deacon said.

Oona considered this, but shook her head. "No. The tower is tall, but nowhere near sixty-seven stories."

Deacon continued to stare up at the tower as Oona peered at the illustration. She read through the words of the announcement again, then returned to the numbers. The answer was in there somewhere.

An idea came to her. She counted the sentences in the announcement.

"Look, Deacon," she said, holding the paper up. She flicked at it with her finger. "See this? See how the announcement is written in lines, like a poem? Each sentence, or part of a sentence, is given its own line."

"I do," said Deacon. He hopped eagerly from one claw to the other.

"There are nine lines," she said, and then ran her finger along the illustration of the tower. "And here we have nine numbers."

"Indeed," Deacon said.

Oona felt a slight tingling sensation just behind her eyes as she ran her finger up the row of numbers, and then back down the rows of sentences. She knew she was onto something.

"I'll bet that these nine numbers refer to the words in these nine sentences," she said.

Deacon began to shake his head, seeing the flaw in her theory. "But what about the number sixty-seven? None of the sentences have sixty-seven words."

"That is true," Oona consented, "but I think I have that figured out as well." She returned the magnifying glass to her pocket, and, after fishing around for a few seconds, pulled out a pencil. "Look here. If we go from the bottom floor of the building to the top, the first number is one."

Oona circled the word *Take,* which was the first word in the first sentence: *Take* the ultimate challenge.

She then circled the second word in the second sentence: Be *the* ultimate hero.

"Take the," Deacon said.

Oona circled the third word in the next sentence: It's the *Magician's* Tower Contest.

She studied the numbers again. 1, 2, 3, 1, 4, 10, 7, 2, 67.

"Here is where the pattern changes," she said, and pointed to the forth number in the sequence: number one again. She circled the first word in the forth line: *Tour* the depths of the mind.

"Take the Magician's Tour," Deacon said, reading the circled words aloud. "What is that?"

"I believe we're about to find out," Oona said, and, following the sequence of numbers, she quickly circled the fourth word in the line that read: Overcome physical tasks *at* risk of life and limb—and the tenth word in: Must be at least thirteen years old to enter *the* tower.

After circling the seventh word in: Winner receives a plaque at the *museum*—and the second word in: (courtesy *of* McMillan's trophy shop)—Oona understood the clue perfectly. And she also realized that her original theory about the last line had been right.

"You were correct, Deacon," Oona said, pointing at the final line with her pencil. "There are not more than sixty-seven letters in the final line, which reads: 'And will go down in magical history.'" She circled the last two words in the sentence. "But there are words six and seven." Beaming at the paper she added: "What say you, Deacon?"

Deacon read: "Take the Magician's Tour at the Museum of Magical History." He paused a moment to consider the clue before exclaiming: "Well done!"

"And now," Oona said, "we know our next destination."

Glancing around, Oona noticed that—with the exception of the architect himself, who sat calmly on the stage reading his newspaper—she was the only person left in the park. A light breeze wound its way through the trees all around her, causing the bells hanging from the gypsy caravan to tinkle playfully against the side of the wagon.

Oona walked toward the caravan, her curiosity getting the better of her.

"Where are you going?" Deacon asked. "The museum is in the opposite direction."

Oona felt a tug of anxiety, but couldn't seem to help herself. Now that there was no one around, it seemed a perfect time to do a little snooping . . . to see if the Punchbowl Oracle thief might have left behind some clue.

"It's all right, Deacon" Oona said. "I've no doubt solved the first clue before anyone else. I'm sure there's time."

Deacon squawked. "Don't be so sure. There are some mighty smart people competing against you."

His tone was harsh, and Oona felt sure that she deserved it. She knew how arrogant her statement must have sounded, but still, Deacon wouldn't have understood her real purpose for wanting to find the thief. He had no idea how terrible it had been for her to lose her mother and sister, and then to be forced to live with the knowledge that it had been her fault.

But what if what Madame Romania from Romania had hinted at was true? she wondered. What if the burden was not hers after all? Oona could not fathom how that could be, but if the punchbowl could show her . . .

"I'm just going to take a few moments," she said, searching the ground as she circled the wagon, "to see if there are any clues."

Deacon shifted restlessly on her shoulder. "This is ridiculous. We are wasting time!"

"Wasting time?" Oona snapped, but then bit her tongue.

"Dear me," Deacon said. He fluttered away from Oona to the ground.

Oona was silent as she scanned the ground, feeling both guilty for having spoken so sharply at Deacon—who she knew had only her best interests in mind—and frustration at finding nothing. At last she straightened, shaking her head.

"Nothing at all." She puffed a strand of hair from her face and then shrugged apologetically at Deacon. "I'm sorry for snapping, Deacon."

The raven stood on the dried ground near one of the caravan wheels. He turned away from her in a clear attempt to show his injured feelings. But after a moment he spoke: "Fine, fine. Water under the bridge. Now can we please get on with the . . . the . . ." He trailed off.

Oona's eyebrows furrowed. "Deacon? What is it?"

Deacon was silent, moving his head about, as if examining something beneath the caravan.

"Deacon?" Oona said.

"It's some sort of trapdoor," he said finally.

Oona squatted down and peered beneath the wagon. Sure enough, she could see precisely what Deacon was referring to. In the bottom of the caravan was a hinged hatch: a second way for someone to have gotten inside. Why a wagon would need such a hatch, she did not know. Beneath the hatch, she could see where the dried mud had been smeared, as if someone had been crawling around down there.

"So that's how they got in," Oona said. "Well spotted, Deacon."

"And look here," Deacon replied, hopping directly beneath the hatch. He poked his beak into the dried mud, jabbing at a shiny object. He managed to pry it out of the ground and then dropped it into Oona's palm.

"It seems that the thief left a bit of evidence," Oona said, surprised. "A silver ring. Look how slim and delicate the design is. See how the jeweler created a heart shape at the top? By the shape and size, Deacon, I would say this is a woman's ring. And quite expensive."

She closed the ring in her fist, stood up straight, and then shoved the evidence into one of her handy skirt pockets.

"Excellent work, Deacon," she said, feeling justified that she had taken the time to snoop. Her mind suddenly raced with possible suspects—it could have been any one of the women from the party last night, or even some-one who had not attended but had sneaked into the park unnoticed. She put her arm out, and Deacon flew to her sleeve.

"Now, my friend," she said, "let's go win this chal-lenge."

CHAPTER FOUR

The Tour

Y ou see, Deacon," Oona said, "there was no need to
hurry. There is no one else here."

The two of them moved quickly up the front
steps to the Museum of Magical History, an enormous
white building that looked more like a stone fortress than
a museum. As she made her way to the top step, Oona
recalled how, only three months ago, a gaggle of girls had
managed to break into this seemingly impenetrable fortress and steal two highly magical daggers—one of which
had been used to turn the Wizard into a toad.

The girls, it turned out, had been none other than the
nine remaining members of the Sisterhood of the Witch,
an ancient coven of witches. Oona had been further

astonished to discover that each of the girls was nearly five hundred years old. Now that Red Martin had gone into hiding, however, the witches no longer had access to his supply of turlock root, the main ingredient in their magical beauty cream, which kept them forever young.

Just how Red Martin was smuggling the root in from Faerie was something that Oona desperately wished to find out. The Glass Gates had barred the passage between the two worlds since the end of the Great Faerie War. More than how he was getting past the gates, however, she wondered where Red Martin himself was now, and what crimes he was concocting. It was Red Martin's own confession to Oona that he had been the mastermind behind her father's death that made her all the more furious to know that the wicked man was still at large.

Oona tugged open the museum door and stepped through. The entryway consisted of a vast circular room with high-beamed ceilings. A ring of massive monolithic stones stood at the center of the room, a perfectly preserved sister set to those known as Stonehenge in England.

Oona approached the uniformed guard at the entrance, a thickset man with meaty arms and no neck. She was pleased to see no one else there. Beside the guard, sitting on a carved wooden pedestal, was a pen and thickly bound registry.

Oona brought the pen to the paper, intending on signing her name to the top of the page, when her breath suddenly froze. There was already a name at the top of the registry: a big, familiar, loopy scrawl that took up nearly four lines.

"Isadora Iree," she read aloud, disbelieving. How was it possible? Isadora had solved the clue and beat her to the museum? It seemed inconceivable. And yet there was the fact of Isadora's signature staring Oona in the face. Perhaps she'd underestimated Isadora's intellect. *Perhaps,* Oona thought, *I've overestimated my own.*

Her breakfast gave an uneasy turn in her stomach.

"I'm here for the Magician's Tour," she said expectantly to the guard.

The guard cocked his thumb toward an easel behind him. The easel supported a sign that read:

MAGICIAN'S TOUR

TIMES

12:30 p.m.

1:00 p.m.

2:00 p.m.

4:00 p.m.

Oona looked at the clock hanging above the guard's head.

"It's twelve thirty-five now," said Deacon. "It appears we'll have to wait for the one o'clock tour."

Oona sighed, and then smiled up at the guard, batting her eyelashes innocently.

"Is it possible that we might . . . join the twelve thirty tour? We're only a few minutes late."

The guard shook his head sternly. "No, miss. I have strict instructions. You'll have to wait for the one o'clock tour."

Oona's lips pinched together, and she could feel the frustration beginning to build. Being forced to wait didn't seem very reasonable to her at all. She was only five minutes late, after all. How much of the tour could she have possibly missed? And the fact that Isadora was already in there, ahead of her . . . it was unacceptable.

"You have only yourself to blame," Deacon said. "If we had come straight here, instead of dillydallying about the gypsy caravan, we would have made the first tour."

Oona bit at her lip to keep from snapping a retort. Of course Deacon was right, but that didn't mean he needed to rub it in her face. And then another voice sounded in her head. It was the soothing voice of her mother. *Worrying doesn't make anything better, Oona. Sometimes there is nothing you can do but wait.*

It wasn't so much a *real* voice in her head as it was a memory: something her mother had said to her on more than one occasion whenever Oona's patience was being put to the test, as it was now.

Oona smoothed out the top of her dress. "This is no problem at all, Deacon," she said calmly. "Isadora is the only one here ahead of us. I'm sure there will be ample time to catch up. And there is no one else here."

She tucked a stray hair back into place, attempting to appear calm and in control, but on the inside she began to feel quite distressed. While it was true that there was no one else yet there, a whole half-hour lead would give Isadora an invaluable advantage, and it was while Oona was wandering anxiously through the tall stone circle that Roderick Rutherford strode through the front entrance, red flyer in hand.

Several minutes later Adler Iree followed him in, as well as—surprise of all surprises—Mr. Bop, the enormously fat man from the Magicians Legal Alliance, who huffed and puffed with the exertion of having just climbed the flight of stairs.

Oona's impatience began to burn. The clock hands ticked away, intolerably slowly, as if someone had put a spell on it. Her thoughts wandered to the ring she had found beneath the caravan. The ladies' ring. She fiddled with it in her pocket, considering whose it might be.

"I was sure I'd see you here, so I was," said Adler Iree in his lilting Irish brogue. He leaned impishly against one of the massive stones. "Well ahead of the pack, you are, Miss Crate."

Oona managed to keep from blushing, but only just. Whether a suspect in a case, or a competitor in a contest, Oona couldn't seem to help the jittery feeling she felt around the boy. He was strong jawed, with large, watchful blue eyes and rosy cheeks lined with intricately patterned symbols.

"Maybe ahead of the pack," Oona said, "but not so much ahead of your sister."

Adler scratched thoughtfully at his head. "Oh, aye. I saw her name at the top of the registry. Makes me wonder, so it does."

"Wonder what?" Oona asked, though she suspected she knew what he was hinting at.

"How she got the clue so fast," Adler said. "The answer, I mean. Isadora's cunning, so she is, but she's no Isaac Newton."

Oona laughed out loud. Sir Isaac Newton was one of her heroes, a man of science, facts, and logical deduction who had lived in the World of Man. Oona's father had owned a book written about the scientist and his work, and Oona had read every word of it, the discoveries of Sir Isaac far more interesting to her than the bland histories of magic that her uncle required her to read as his apprentice.

"How did you enjoy your summer holiday?" Oona asked.

Adler shrugged. "Oh, New York's all right, but I prefer Dark Street, so I do. The people here are so much more . . . interesting." His smile flashed, and Oona blushed.

"I've read all about New York, of course," Oona said, shielding her hands behind her back to hide her sudden jitters. "But I've never been there."

Adler's eyebrows rose in surprise. "Never been to the World of Man?"

Oona shook her head, feeling quite foolish. The Iron Gates were so close, yet as curious as she was, she had never ventured across. "My uncle is the Wizard, and I am his apprentice. He feels that our place is here, on Dark Street. After all, it is the Wizard's responsibility to protect the World of Man from faerie attack, should the Glass Gates ever be reopened."

Adler looked thoughtful. "But don't you think you should know what you're protecting?"

Oona nodded appreciatively. "That does sound quite logical."

Adler laughed, and for an instant Oona didn't know if she should feel embarrassed or pleased.

"I like how you talk, Miss Crate," he said.

Oona swallowed a lump in her throat. This cute boy liked how she talked, and she was forced to suppress a smile. It was the most wonderful thing he could have said. She was tempted to tell him that she liked how he talked, too—as well as his hands, and his face, and his mysterious tattoos—but she couldn't quite get herself to say it.

She bit nervously at her bottom lip, and then said: "That was some clue the architect put together."

"Sure was," Adler said. "I almost missed the whole thing because of reading the numbers the wrong way. Which is why I'm so surprised Isadora could have figured it out so fast. I always wanted to play riddle games when we were younger, but she hated them. Just didn't have the mind for them."

"Speak of the devil," Oona said, and pointed across the entrance hall.

"And so the devil appears," replied Isadora, flashing her eyes tauntingly as she emerged through an arched doorway, and then walked right past Oona and Adler, holding a golden token high in the air. Oona folded her arms, and Adler shook his head as if in disbelief.

Isadora stopped at the front door, where Roderick Rutherford stood beaming his handsome white teeth at her.

"Look, Roderick," Isadora said. She held the token up like a trophy. "I'm the first one through."

"Bravo," Roderick said. "You'd better hurry, my lady.

Our tour is about to begin, and you've still got the physical challenge ahead of you. We might catch up."

"Look, everyone," Isadora said, grinning broadly, "I'm in the lead. See?"

She pointed to the token. Light glinted off its gold surface like a tiny sun.

"Enjoy the tour," she said, her voice dripping with sarcasm. "It's dreadfully long, and even more dreadfully boring. Ta-ta."

She pushed through the door and was gone, headed for the second challenge of the day. Oona's frustration began to burn. With a half-hour lead, it was more than likely that Isadora Iree would be the first contestant to finish the day's challenges. Oona instantly regretted taking time to snoop about the caravan.

"Well," said Adler, "let's hope the physical challenge will be more difficult than the mental one. She's not very athletic, my sister. We just might have time to catch up. Ah, look, here's our tour guide now."

Twenty minutes later, Oona was ready to scream with impatience as the tour guide droned on like a monotonous wind through a hollow cave.

"Here we have an artist's rendition of how Dark Street

might have appeared six or seven hundred years ago, in the time of the Magicians of Old, before the closing of the Glass Gates." The tour guide, a hunched-over elderly man who smelled of moldy cloth, gestured toward a large painting on the wall. It depicted an age long past, when humans and faeries walked the street together.

Oona squeezed her hands impatiently, fingernails digging into her palms. The tour had been inching its way through the museum, and Oona was growing more nervous with each agonizing minute. She had never known twenty minutes to have ever passed so slowly. No doubt Isadora Iree had already made it past the second challenge, and was basking in her victory at that very moment.

The intolerably slow-moving tour guide leaned precariously on his cane, and intoned: "I'm sure you are all aware that Dark Street is the last of the Faerie roads, leading from the World of Man to the Land of Faerie."

Oona rolled her eyes and twirled her hand in a yes-yes-we-know-all-of-this-please-hurry-it-up sort of gesture.

The tour guide took no notice. "The Great Faerie Wars, 1300 to 1313, is said to have begun when the five greatest Magicians of Old stole an ancient book known as *Malgoule-Morgoth-DeMilmim* from the Faerie Royal Treasury. With the knowledge they gained from the book, the magicians' powers grew quite rapidly. Nonetheless, when the Queen of Faerie learned of the humans' treachery, the great magical war began. The magicians were able to fend off the queen's armies for thirteen years, until the closing of twelve of the Faerie roads, and the construction of the Iron and Glass Gates upon the final, thirteenth road—which henceforth became known as Dark Street. The magicians then pooled their magic into a single source—Pendulum House—and then chose a single individual to act as the keeper of the house's powers. That person became known as the first Wizard, whose job it is to use the house's magic to defend the World of Man in the event of a faerie attack. Who the first Wizard was is a matter of much debate."

The tour guide paused to catch his breath, and Oona felt she was about to go out of her mind with boredom. This was information every five-year-old born on Dark Street could recite. She heaved an exasperated sigh.

"Patience," Deacon whispered in her ear.

"It was Oswald the Great," the tour guide continued after patting his forehead with a handkerchief, "the most powerful of the Magicians of Old, who is credited with closing the Glass Gates and severing the two worlds completely."

The guide pointed at a painting to his right, and Oona thought she could hear the creak of the old man's bones.

"And here is a portrait of Oswald's famous magic wand, painted by the equally famous painter Bernard T. Slyhand. It was Slyhand himself who stole Oswald's wand and then afterward sent this painting to Oswald, along with a ransom note demanding a great deal of gold." The old man lowered his hand to a glass-encased piece of red parchment below the painting. "Oswald never received the painting, or the note. In fact, Oswald was never seen again. No one knows what became of the mighty magician, just as no one knows what became of the stolen wand—though legend has it that the wand itself is the only key to the Glass Gates."

Oona felt like she might scream. Who cared about Bernard T. Slyhand and this stupid painting of Oswald's wand? Especially when Isadora Iree was out there right now, victory in her grasp. Glancing around at her fellow competitors, she saw that Roderick Rutherford appeared just as bored as she was, though Mr. Bop, who was standing closest to the old tour guide, appeared rapt with attention.

Adler's and Oona's eyes met. He gave a little yawn, followed by a barely discernable smile.

"And that," said the tour guide, "is the end of our tour. For those in the contest, I've been instructed to give you each one of these. You are to take it to the tower."

He reached into his pocket and slowly removed a handful of golden tokens, holding them out in a shaky open hand.

"We hope you enjoyed this trip through history," he

said, his voice aquiver with age, "and if you have any questions, I would be more than happy to answer—"

But Oona didn't hear the rest of what the old tour guide had to say. She snatched a token from his hand and bolted for the front entrance so quickly that Deacon leapt from her shoulder and followed by flight.

"No running in the . . . ," the security guard called after her as she banged through the front door. She could hear Roderick and Adler hot on her heels as she plunged down the front steps, and then darted up the sidewalk in the direction of Oswald Park.

"Here I come, Isadora," she said under her breath.

Her shoes pounded the pavement, weaving through clusters of confused-looking pedestrians, many of whom clasped red flyers in their hands. Lungs beginning to burn, she sprinted up the sidewalk with all the speed she could muster. To her left, the iron fence separating the park from the street flew by, seemingly endless. Oona had never realized just how large the park was. Twice she nearly tripped on her skirt. At the park entrance she could feel herself beginning to slow, and by the time she reached the first row of oak trees, Roderick had over- taken her lead.

"Bloody dress!" she said through her ragged breath, though she knew that it was not simply the dress that was slowing her, but that Roderick was stronger and faster.

Stronger physically, she thought to herself as they cut across the grass toward the tower. *But stronger mentally? I think not.*

She could hear Adler Iree clomping across fallen leaves behind her, but as they neared the tower, Oona was fairly certain she was going to beat him. Roderick was the first to clamor up the steps to the stage, where the architect stood patiently waiting. There was no sign of Isadora.

"Here!" said Roderick, slapping his golden token into the architect's outstretched hand and pressing his other hand against his side.

"Your task," said the architect, "is to retrieve a golden banana from inside the tower and make your way to the door marked 'exit.' You may now enter the tower." The stubby-legged little man paused briefly before adding, with no small grin: "At your own risk."

Roderick nodded as if he understood. He did not immediately make his way to the door, however, but took a moment to catch his breath.

"What are you waiting for, Roderick?" a voice shouted, and as Oona approached the architect with her own token, she glanced toward the crowd of spectators who had once again formed near the stage. The shouting voice was that of Roderick's father, Sir Baltimore. His face was apple red. "Get a move on, boy! You have a race to win!"

Roderick glanced in his father's direction as Oona handed her token to the architect, receiving the same instructions as Roderick. "Your task is to retrieve a golden banana from inside the tower and make your way to the door marked 'exit.' You may now enter the tower . . . at your own risk."

She saw a glimmer of mischievous delight in the man's eyes and instantly began to wonder just what she was getting herself into. What twisted game did the architect have waiting for them behind that door?

Deacon landed on Oona's shoulder, ruffling his feathers as if ready to settle in.

"The bird must wait out here," the architect added to Oona before Adler Iree stepped up behind her and handed over his token.

As the architect gave Adler the same instructions he had given Oona and Roderick, Oona cocked her head to one side and shrugged. "Sorry, Deacon. Guess I'm on my own in there."

Deacon cast a menacing look toward the architect, puffing himself up, as if to say: *If anything happens to her . . .*

"It's all right, Deacon. I'll manage," Oona said, her breath slowly returning to normal.

"As you wish," Deacon said, and flew to the nearest tree branch, cawing his displeasure.

"I said get a move on, Roderick!" Sir Baltimore shouted at his son.

The three of them, Oona, Adler, and Roderick, approached the crooked tower door together. Oona craned her neck back, peering up at the swaying monstrosity, wondering how high they would be required to climb today, and what dreamed-up obstacles the architect had placed in there.

Then came a scream. It pierced through the tower walls like something from a nightmare, followed by what might have been shrieks of high-pitched laughter. Oona went all over with goose bumps.

Roderick took in a startled breath. "Isadora!" he shouted, before wrenching open the door and darting inside. "I'll save you, my lady!"

Adler and Oona watched him go.

Oona remembered her own hasty promise to Isadora: *I won't use any magic at all during the contest, and then we shall see who is the better.*

It had been a silly thing to agree to; she had known that from the moment the words had left her lips, but she also felt it was her duty not to go back on her vow. She had a surprisingly clear memory of her father saying something like: "A great man is only as good as his word." And Oona's mother replied: "And a great woman, as well." Her father had nodded his agreement, and then Oona had said: "And a great girl!" Her parents had laughed. "Quite right, Oona, dear. Quite right," her father had replied, mussing up her hair as he did so.

Father made it to the final challenge, and he hadn't needed magic, Oona thought. *And neither do I.*

That settled the matter.

Another scream issued from the half-open doorway. Oona's throat was suddenly very dry as she and Adler followed Roderick into the tower.

CHAPTER FIVE

Up Through the Ape House

G et these beasts away from me!" Isadora howled.

The chatter and shrieks of chimpanzees filled Oona's ears. The chimps seemed to be everywhere, chattering, chortling, throwing things.

Oona, Roderick, and Adler bolted for the nearest shelter: a wooden table covered with banana peels and half-eaten apples.

A ripe red tomato collided with the side of Oona's head as she dove beneath the table.

"Ouch!" Roderick cried, sliding in beside Oona and digging something small and hard from his collar. "That was an avocado pit," he said. "Might as well be throwing stones."

"That's nothing," Adler said, and then held up a foot-long fish. "This hit me square in the face, so it did."

Oona was suddenly worried about what else the chimps might throw.

"We appear to be in some sort of monkey house," Roderick said.

"You don't say," Adler replied sarcastically.

"Actually, they are apes," Oona said. "Chimpanzees, to be precise. Not monkeys. I've read about them."

"What's the difference?" asked Adler.

Oona frowned. "Well, I'm not sure. But I think apes are usually much bigger than monkeys . . . and stronger."

"And smellier," said Adler. He squinched up his nose.

Oona had to agree. The room smelled terrible.

"How did Isadora get way up there?" Roderick asked, cocking his thumb toward the ceiling.

Unsure of what he meant, Oona peeked out from beneath the table.

The tower walls rose up around them like a house of cards built by an unsteady hand. The four walls leaned awkwardly in different directions, yet somehow they managed to meet the high-beamed ceiling three dizzying stories overhead.

Oona and the two boys were currently in some sort of kitchen area on the bottom floor, where an enormous wood-burning stove sat in the center of the room, atop of which bubbled an equally large kettle of steaming liquid.

The floor above them—which was not really a floor at all, because there *was* no floor to speak of—was made up entirely of various pieces of floating furniture. Oona blinked in surprise, unsure of what she was seeing.

The furnishings appeared to hover in the air, with no support from underneath, and her first thought was that some sort of spell had been placed on them. But upon further examination she realized that the furniture was actually suspended by long black ropes that hung down from the high ceiling.

So far as she could make out, there were two upper levels, one above the other, with a series of steps and platforms built into the walls that led from one level to the next.

The first level consisted of a sofa, a chandelier, a frighteningly heavy-looking grand piano, and an even heavier-looking red brick fireplace complete with chimney. Oona shook her head, somewhat surprised to see that the fireplace was fully lit. Bits of ash and spark rained down to the lower level of the room as the fireplace rocked back and forth on the straining ropes.

Farther up, on the topmost level, a second line of furniture also hung from the ceiling, swaying slightly from side to side on their flimsy ropes like bizarre pendulums:

a standing oil lamp, a four-poster bed, a chest of drawers, and a mirrored dressing table. At the very top of the room, nearest to the hanging lamp, a rickety landing stuck out of the wall like a crooked wooden finger. It led to a bright red door, and from Oona's vantage point three stories below, she was just able to make out the word EXIT marked on the door in fat white letters.

Further examination of the steps and platforms along the walls revealed that the stairs leading from the bottom level to the second were on one side of the room, while the steps that rose from the second level to the third were on the opposite side. This posed quite a problem—how to get from one side of the room to the other with no floor to walk on—though presently Oona realized this was the least of their worries.

The apes, which were making so much noise that Oona wished to stuff her fingers into her ears, could all be found on the upper levels. They swung from the ropes and dangled from the edges of the furniture like extremely hairy lunatics. Oona counted five of them, and they seemed to be everywhere at once, causing the ropes holding up the piano to creak, or bouncing on the sofa like a trampoline.

Oona could see Isadora up there on the sofa, looking fearfully disheveled and holding on for dear life.

"Someone get me down from here!" she cried.

The apes screamed with laughter as several of the chimps joined in on the fun of bouncing around Isadora and the piles of fruit on the sofa.

Something shiny caught Oona's gaze: something hanging from the end of a thin chain around the neck of one of the chimps. It was hard to tell, because of how feverishly the hairy beast was bouncing on the sofa cushion beside Isadora, but to Oona the shiny object looked vaguely like a crescent of gold. With a quick glance at the chimp's companions, she realized that each of the apes had a similar necklace.

The golden bananas, she thought. *That's what the architect told us to retrieve.*

She also realized that when the apes weren't busy throwing food at the contestants, they were attempting to toss it into the boiling pot. At present, one of the chimps, a large, fierce-looking one with a stripe of gray across its eyes, was preparing to toss one of Isadora's shoes into the boiling stew below, but when the ape caught sight of Oona peeking out from beneath the table, it hurled the shoe at her instead, striking her in the forehead.

"Bloody beast!" Oona shouted, rubbing at her forehead and ducking back beneath the table.

"Roderick!" Isadora cried from above. "I thought you were my BOYFRIEND!"

"I am, my lady," Roderick called back.

"Then get out here, BOYFRIEND! Now! Retrieve my shoe, and then get me out of here!"

Roderick looked pale. "Just a . . . a . . . a minute, my lady!"

"I'll just a minute you, BOYFRIEND," Isadora howled, "and . . . hey, let go of my hair, you evil thing!"

This was followed by a fit of high-pitched chimpanzee chortling.

Oona tapped both boys on the shoulder. "Here's what I believe we have to do. First we'll need to climb the stairs along the wall to get to the next level. Once we get there we will have to hop from one piece of furniture to the next in order to get across to the other side of the room. From there we can travel up the second set of steps to the top level, and again hop across the furniture to the exit. The golden bananas are hanging from the necks of the apes. We'll each need to get close enough to one of them in order to take a banana."

"I know what to do!" Roderick snapped at her. "You don't need to tell me."

He leapt from beneath the table and made a dash for the opposite end of the room, toward the stairs leading to the second level. Fruit rained down on him from all directions, and Oona wanted to cover her ears against the manic cry of the apes. But instead of cowering beneath the table, she followed Roderick, hoping that his lead would draw most of the fire.

It worked . . . sort of.

Roderick took the stairs three at a time, swatting back potatoes and bananas. For the second time, a tomato struck Oona in the back of the head. She stumbled forward, nearly losing her balance as the juices splattered through her hair and oozed down her back.

"You nasty beasts!" she shouted, but quickly realized that she had been the lucky one when a ripe, red beet hammered Roderick between the eyes. The beet cracked open against his head, spinning him down against the wall just as he reached the second-floor platform.

For an instant Oona thought it had split Roderick's head right open, but kneeling down to see if he was all right, she saw that it was not blood after all, but only purplish beet juice that blobbed down his nose.

Realizing that he was going to be okay, Oona seized her chance to take the lead. The first platform jutted out about six feet from the wall and then stopped, where a three-foot gap opened between the platform's edge and the arm of the hanging sofa. Knowing that a single hesitation might cause her to lose her nerve completely, Oona jumped. But not far enough. Her foot caught on the arm of the sofa, and she tumbled into Isadora's lap.

Isadora let out a sharp scream of surprise.

The ropes creaked as the sofa swung from side to side like a boat caught in a storm.

"Get off me!" Isadora shouted, swatting blindly at both Oona and the two apes that were presently tying bits of banana peel into her golden hair. Oona shoved a pile of fruit out of the way and sat up, careful not to lean too far forward.

Suddenly, the sofa gave a jerk sideways as Roderick landed on the cushion beside her, and for one heart-stopping second Oona was sure that the ropes were about to break and the entire sofa was going to crash to the bottom floor. But the ropes held, creaking under the added weight as Oona pulled her feet up, meaning to crawl over Isadora. But Roderick grabbed hold of Oona's skirt, pulling her back into her seat.

Oona gasped. "Whatever happened to chivalry, Mr. Rutherford?" she chided.

Roderick did not answer, but stepped impolitely over her and caught hold of one of the apes by the arm. He pulled the golden banana from its neck, and the chain snapped off quite easily. He then attempted to push the chimpanzee away, but the chimp was far stronger than Roderick. It picked him up by his arm, seemingly with no effort at all, and dangled him over the edge of the sofa.

"BOYFRIEND!" Isadora shouted, attempting to swat

the second monkey away. "What are you doing? Get this beast off me!"

"I'm a little busy, Isadora," he called back, clinging precariously to the ape's hairy arm.

"Whoooooa!"

The sound shot from his lips as the ape tossed him through the air toward a fellow chimp on the piano. Roderick somersaulted over the chandelier, and the piano ape caught him by the back of his cloak before fervently tossing him back to the ape on the sofa. This went on for several more throws before both apes became bored with the game, and Roderick came down with a resounding *GONG!* on top of the piano.

Meanwhile, down below, Adler was having difficulty getting past the stripe-faced ape, which had descended to the bottom floor and was blocking his way to the stairs.

"Roderick!" Isadora crooned. "Come back here and help me!"

But Roderick was busy pushing himself to his feet on top of the piano lid. He glanced up toward the next level of furniture, and said: "I have an idea!"

Oona pulled her feet back onto the sofa and began to crawl over Isadora. Roderick may have taken the lead, but she didn't plan on letting him keep it.

"Where do you think you're going?" Isadora asked.

"Isadora, why don't you—" but Oona was rudely cut

short when one of the apes grabbed her around the waist and tossed her in the direction of the piano. Skirts flying like a wind-filled flag, she cartwheeled through the air, completely out of control.

To her dismay, the chimp on the piano was presently throwing a handful of dried prunes at Adler, and thus failed to catch her before she slammed down on the piano top. Her shoe clanged against the keyboard, and for one panicky instant her breath was knocked from her body, but a moment later she pushed herself to her knees and the pungent air filled her lungs. The fall had shaken her, to be sure, but, checking herself over, she seemed remarkably unharmed.

Ahead of her, Roderick leapt from the piano to the hanging fireplace, but seemed to misjudge the distance. He only just managed to catch hold of the mantelpiece and save himself from a nine-foot fall. His feet swung forward into the fire, but he quickly pulled himself up onto the chimp-free chimney. From there he hopped to the platform on the other side and began rapidly making his way up the steps to the third level.

"BOYFRIEND!" Isadora cried. "You better not leave me here!"

"Hold your horses, my lady!" Roderick called back.

Oona took her footing on the piano rather precariously. Her shoes had little grip, and they were sliding all over the place. She steadied herself on one of the ropes, waiting on the lip of the lid as the piano rocked closer to the fireplace.

She leapt . . . but like Roderick, she jumped too early. For half a heartbeat she thought she was going to fly right into the mouth of the fireplace, but her fingers clamped hold of the mantle. She kicked her feet, fighting to pull herself up. Her dress felt like it weighed two hundred pounds.

Suddenly, there was an ape above her, this one more gray than black, and it cackled at her with wild amusement. It caught hold of the back of her dress, hauling her up. Oona had an idea that the chimp's intentions were not so much to help her but to start up its own little game of Toss the Helpless Girl.

Just as the ape brought her up to chimney height, however, both Oona and the ape realized that something was burning . . . and a second later Oona *felt* what it was. The bottom of her dress had swung into the flames and was now on fire.

Dreadfully fearful of the flames, the gray ape tossed her in the opposite direction of the piano, but not before Oona reached out and caught hold of the golden banana hanging from its neck. The chain snapped, and she came down on the far platform, rolling over several times before hitting the wall. She quickly sat up, slapping at the hem of her dress, only to realize that the fire had been doused in her roll across the floor.

"Well," she said, breathing a sigh of relief. "That was certainly memorable."

"Isadora!" Oona heard Roderick shout from above. "Grab hold. I'll pull you up!"

Pushing herself to her feet, Oona glanced toward the second level of furniture. She could see Roderick up there balancing on the hanging chest of drawers. He steadied himself with one rope and was using his other hand to rock the chandelier below toward Isadora.

It took only two swings, and Isadora grabbed hold. She hung on for dear life as the ape on the sofa tried its best to pull her free. But the chimp quickly gave up and started throwing the sofa cushions at Adler, who had only just managed to reach the stairs at the bottom of the tower.

Suddenly, the entrance to the tower swung inward, and Mr. Bop stepped into the ape house, causing the entire structure to quake with each step. A fresh round of fruits and vegetables began to pelt the enormous man about the head, and he quickly backed out through the door, apparently having second thoughts about his chances in the physical task.

Oona, meanwhile, raced up the steps to the top floor, determined to beat Roderick and Isadora to the door on the far side of the room.

Two grinning-faced apes blocked her way at the top of the stairs. How Roderick had managed to get past them, she didn't have a clue, but she could see him now, hauling Isadora up to the third floor, Isadora clinging to the chandelier with her eyes shut, her shoeless feet dangling beneath her. She was about halfway up, and Oona realized that there was no time to waste.

Remembering her recent encounter with the gray-colored chimp on the chimney, she reached into her pocket and pulled out a red phosphorus match. The two chimpanzees unfolded their lanky arms and watched with growing interest as Oona struck the match along the wall, and then both of them jumped back.

She held the match out before her.

The chimps shrieked and shrank back from the flame. One of them actually covered his eyes in a see-no-evil impression that, under different circumstances, Oona might have found funny. The match extinguished itself as she hurried past the apes. She flicked it toward the bottom floor, where it became one more ingredient in the bubbling kettle three stories below.

She reached the end of the platform at a run and leapt for the dressing table. Catching sight of her reflection in the attached mirror, her first thought was: *I look dreadful.* Her second thought, however, was: *I'm going to crash right into it.*

Sure enough, she slammed into the mirror, cracking it down the middle and making the table swing in a perilous arc. She clung desperately to the mirror, and Roderick nearly lost his balance as the table bumped against the edge of the neighboring chest of drawers.

"Don't you drop me, BOYFRIEND!" Isadora howled.

Roderick managed to keep his grip, and a second later Isadora was there with him, atop the chest of drawers. Oona jumped to join them. Her landing caused the chest of drawers to swing sideways, throwing Isadora and Roderick into the air, and the two of them tumbled onto the huge four-poster bed.

"Roderick!" Isadora snapped, pushing him off of her. "This is highly inappropriate."

"I beg your pardon?" he said, shaking his head.

"I thought you were going to be chivalrous!" she said.

Noticing for the first time that the two of them were sharing the same bed, his mouth began to pop open and close. "But my lady, I assure you, I had no such intention."

"A likely story," she said.

"Really," said Roderick, "it wasn't my fault."

"Then whose fault was it?" she asked dubiously.

"It was . . . hers!" he exclaimed as Oona leapt onto the bed and then dashed across the covers toward the hanging lamp on the other side.

"Quick!" Roderick shouted. "She's going to win!"

Like a monkey on a vine, Oona caught hold of the lamp and sailed across the remaining space to the wooden landing. With her feet planted firmly on the edge, she let the lamp swing back toward the bed and turned to make her way to the exit. But something was there, impeding her way. It was that rascally stripe-faced chimp.

"How did you get up here?" Oona asked.

Stripe-face lunged for her. Oona ducked and spun around, but Stripe-face caught hold of her dress, plunging his hand into her pocket. A second later Oona was free, but when she glanced back, she saw that the monkey had something in its hand. Something small and shiny silver.

It was the ring! The evidence she had found beneath the caravan.

For a long moment Oona was torn. She glanced at the door marked EXIT and then back to the ring in the grinning ape's hand. Victory was in her grasp, she knew . . . but the evidence . . . the case.

Her eyes narrowed.

"Give that back, you little thief!" Oona shouted, and started after the ape.

Stripe-face leapt the distance between the landing and the bed in a single bound. Oona followed suit, nearly bouncing off the end of the bed when she landed. Grabbing hold of Stripe-face's arm, she just managed to stay bed bound, but the golden banana she had taken from the gray monkey fell from her hand and bounced right across the bed to land at Isadora's feet. Isadora greedily snatched it up, and now both she and Roderick were the only ones with bananas.

But Oona had no time to think. She leapt on the chimp, trying to force the ring from its vicelike grip. The ape snapped at her with its large teeth, the two of them wrestling on the bed. Something flashed in Oona's eyes, and she realized it was the golden banana around the ape's neck.

Oona grabbed hold and yanked, and at the same time shouted: *"Ignigtis!"*

A ball of flame appeared in front of the ape's face, and the chimp's expression turned instantly from one of menace to that of horror. It dropped the ring on the bed and bounded away across the room, swinging wildly from rope to rope until it was as far away from Oona and the floating flame as possible.

Oona felt instantly guilty. While she knew that there was no rule against using magic in the contest, she had broken her word to Isadora. Yet it had been the thought of losing a crucial bit of evidence—evidence that could possibly lead her to the punchbowl—that had caused her to do it, not because she had wanted to gain some unfair advantage in order to win.

She picked up the ring, and then the fire—which had been nothing more than an illusion and could not have hurt the monkey even if it had stuck its hairy hand into it—winked out. She repocketed the ring before quickly realizing that both Roderick and Isadora were no longer on the bed.

While this realization brought with it a sense of relief that Isadora might not have witnessed Oona's use of magic, it also brought a panicky comprehension that she had fallen behind in the race. She glanced around in time to see Isadora and Roderick hurrying along the landing toward the exit, Roderick in the lead.

Heart pounding in her chest, Oona grabbed hold of the lamp and swung across to the landing. Up ahead, Roderick stopped. He opened the door and then stepped aside, extending his hand.

"Ladies first," he said, allowing Isadora to exit ahead of him.

"How very chivalrous," Isadora said, and stepped through the open doorway, where Oona could see the architect himself outside on a platform, waiting to congratulate today's winner. Isadora received something that looked like a blue piece of ribbon as Roderick stepped through the door after her to receive a pat on the back, and what looked like a red ribbon of his own.

By the time Oona stepped through the threshold, a

cool breeze was sweeping across the outside platform. The fresh air was a reward in itself . . . but still, she couldn't help but feel cheated somehow.

"Good show," she heard the architect say. She showed him the golden banana she had taken from the stripe-faced ape, and he shoved something into her hand: a short bit of white ribbon. Oona smiled politely and nodded, though truthfully she felt like balling the ribbon up and tossing it to the crowd three stories below.

Five minutes later, Adler came huffing through the exit, his threadbare cloak looking even worse for wear, though remarkably his top hat remained firmly stationed atop his head, as if it had been glued there. He approached the architect, exchanging his golden banana for a green-colored ribbon, and then grinned at Oona. But presently, Oona did not feel much like grinning back.

Isadora Iree, however, was beaming.

CHAPTER SIX

The Academy of Fine Young Ladies

T hird place!"

Chin in hands, Oona sat in the Pendulum House grand parlor, her back to the crackling fireplace. A tall, windowless room with large tapestries depicting sprites, and goblins, and gnomes, it was one of Oona's favorite places to think. She enjoyed the way the creatures in the artwork moved when people weren't looking at them, so that the magical figures never appeared in the same position twice.

Just as peculiar was the enormous seven-foot-tall pendulum that swung through the center of the room. It was this spectacular oddity from whence Pendulum House took its name, and was the instrument that kept Dark Street moving in perfect time through the Drift.

"Third place," Oona said again. She shook her head disbelievingly and stared at the bit of ribbon in her hand. "And I would have been first, Deacon, had it not been for that infernal monkey-brained monkey stealing the evidence from my pocket."

"Monkey-brained monkey is a redundancy." Deacon stood rigidly on the arm of the sofa. "And besides, I thought you said it was an ape?"

"You know, Deacon," Oona said, "there is little doubt in my mind that Isadora Iree is cheating."

Deacon shook his head. "Cheating? How is that possible? Are you sure you're not just being a poor sport?"

"Poor sport? Me?" she asked.

Deacon shrugged. "All I am saying is that I see no way Miss Iree *could* cheat. If indeed, as you have explained, she used her powers of femininity to get Roderick Rutherford to help her in the physical task, there is no rule in the contest against it. In fact, some might even consider it a virtue."

"Virtue?" Oona asked.

"Am I not speaking clearly?" Deacon asked earnestly.

Oona jumped to her feet, unconvinced. "But it is not the physical task I am concerned with. Rather the mental task."

"Perhaps you do not give the girl enough credit," Deacon said.

This made Oona want to laugh. She was sure that Isadora would stop at nothing to get exactly what she wanted. Oona removed the ring they had found from her pocket, holding it up to the firelight.

"Perhaps you are right, Deacon," she said, and began pacing the floor, moving in rhythm to the swing of the pendulum. "Perhaps Isadora is more clever than I would like to admit. After all, it is quite a coincidence, is it not, that the night before Isadora Iree claims victory in the first challenge, a very powerful object goes missing from the gypsy caravan? A tool that can be used to answer any question."

"If you are speaking of the Punchbowl Oracle, I must repeat that there is no mention of it in the *Encyclopedia Arcanna*. It is highly unlikely that a bowl with the powers to answer any question would exist without being included in the encyclopedia."

Oona spun around. "Improbable, but not impossible! Let us theorize, Deacon. If Isadora did steal the punchbowl, she could then use it to ask something like: 'Oh, magic punchbowl, what is the answer to the first mental challenge?' and the answer would appear before her in the bowl. How else do you explain Isadora getting the answer and showing up at the museum before anyone else? And don't say she just figured it out, Deacon. This is Isadora Iree we're talking about."

Deacon opened his beak as if to protest, but then appeared to reconsider. "Yes, I see your point."

"And this, too, Deacon," she said, holding up the ring. "A ladies' ring, found beneath the trapdoor to the caravan. Do you remember if Isadora was wearing a ring the night of the party?"

Deacon shook his head.

"No," Oona said. "I can't remember either."

"You could show her the ring and ask her if she lost it," Deacon suggested.

Oona stopped pacing, her expression brightening. "An excellent idea, Deacon! Let's do it tonight."

"Tonight?" asked Deacon. "But don't you think it smarter to spend your time trying to figure out that clue?"

He pointed his beak at the white ribbon, which Oona had left on the sofa. She could see the words written on it in black ink.

Deacon hopped to the sofa cushion and picked the ribbon up with a talon. "The architect gave it to the four remaining contestants to give them a head start on the challenge facing you all tomorrow," he said.

"He did indeed," Oona said, taking the ribbon from Deacon and reading the clue.

Go see the RAIN AIR EVENT
Ask for the PRICE ON UP

Take it to the STREAM of SNOT HAUNTED faces
At the Dark EARTH TREE TEST

Oona nodded. "Yes Deacon, I believe you are right."

"You mean that you should spend this evening concentrating on that clue?" he asked.

Oona favored him with a roguish smile. "No, Deacon. I meant that this evening would be the perfect time to confront Isadora Iree. In fact, there's no time like the present. Samuligan!" she called.

The faerie servant opened the door to the parlor, as if he had been waiting just outside the room. His cowboy boots clicked against the floor, hollow and haunting.

"Will you bring the carriage around?" Oona asked. "We're going to make a little trip to the Academy of Fine Young Ladies."

"But what about the clue?" Deacon asked, and Oona could hear the disapproval in his voice.

"Deacon, if Isadora Iree is indeed the punchbowl thief, then it's likely that even if I do figure out this clue, Isadora will have the answer already. So you see, it is vital that we find her out for the thieving cheat that she is."

"Or the thieving cheat she is not," Deacon said. "I hope you are prepared for that possibility as well."

Thirty minutes later Samuligan pulled the carriage

to a stop in front of the Academy of Fine Young Ladies. The ornate building gleamed prettily in the streetlight as Oona exited the riding compartment and knocked on the front entrance. The door was answered by a rail-thin woman whose gaunt face and high cheekbones gave her a skeletal appearance.

"May I help you?" she inquired, her voice low and disapproving.

Deacon whispered in Oona's ear: "That is Arianna Duvet, headmistress of the academy."

Oona nodded, smiling politely. "Hello, Headmistress Duvet. I'm dreadfully sorry to call so late, but I was wondering if I might have a word with Isadora Iree."

Headmistress Duvet stared down the sides of her nose at Oona, and her mouth pulled into a line so thin it nearly disappeared altogether. "And what is this inappropriately late visit about?" she asked.

Oona wetted her lips. The headmistress made her feel all-over nervous. "It is regarding something I believe Isadora lost. I found it, and would like to return it to her."

Headmistress Duvet raised one well-plucked eyebrow, and Oona noticed for the first time that the eye beneath the brow was not real, but made of glass. And now that Oona watched them, she could see the woman's eyes moving independently of each other.

The headmistress extended her hand. "Give the found object to me, and I will see that it finds its way back to Miss Iree."

Oona frowned. The whole point of this expedition was to see Isadora's reaction to the ring, and she wasn't about to just hand over a crucial piece of evidence, no matter how sternly this woman glared down her nose at her.

Looking the headmistress squarely in her good eye, Oona said: "It is a private matter."

The headmistress looked as if Oona had just given her the worst insult imaginable, and for a moment Oona was afraid that the glass eye might pop right out of her head.

"What is a private matter?" asked a voice from behind Oona. She turned, blinking in surprise. Dressed in an extravagant blue velvet dress, Isadora's mother, Madame Iree, sauntered into the glow of the nearby streetlight. She smiled gracefully at Oona, patting absently at her hair.

"Ah, Madame Iree," said Headmistress Duvet, still looking menacingly at Oona. Oona flinched as the headmistress arrowed a finger at her. "This girl claims to have something of your daughter's. But she will not reveal what it is."

"Well, isn't that convenient?" said Madame Iree, who seemed oblivious to Headmistress Duvet's maniacal stare. "I just happen to be stopping by to visit with Isadora as we speak." She turned to Oona. "Why don't you come up with me, and we can visit her in her room . . . ah, Miss Crate, is it?"

Oona nodded, unable to conceal a smile. Things were working out better than planned. She'd expected at most that Headmistress Duvet would call Isadora to the front door, but here was Madame Iree inviting Oona to visit Isadora's room. It would be the perfect opportunity to see if Isadora happened to have a certain punchbowl sitting out in the open.

Headmistress Duvet eyed Deacon, either unable or unwilling to hide her distain. Her top lip quivered slightly as she said: "The bird must wait outside."

Oona glanced at Deacon, who appeared relieved. She couldn't blame him. Headmistress Duvet was more than a little creepy.

"Good luck," he whispered before flying to the top of the carriage to wait with Samuligan.

"Shall we?" asked Madame Iree, and under the severe gaze of Headmistress Duvet's cross-eyed stare, she and Oona entered the academy, removing their hats and hanging them on hooks in the front entryway.

A long-handled cane leaned ominously against the wall beneath the hooks. The end of the cane expanded out like a paddle, and a single word had been etched into the wood. In thick, easily readable letters it read: IMPROPER. Oona could only imagine the countless stings that paddle had sent through many a fine young lady's backside.

"I'm busy with lesson plans," said Headmistress Duvet, picking up the cane and slapping it in her open palm with a raw *smack*. Both Oona and Madame Iree jumped. "I believe you know the way," the headmistress said, and then turned abruptly and marched down the hall before disappearing into one of the open rooms. Oona felt her shoulders relax.

"This way," said Madame Iree, and began making her way toward a large curved staircase. It reminded Oona of the staircase in Pendulum House, except that these stairs were impeccably well taken care of. The carpets were dazzlingly clean, and the chandelier hanging in the entryway sparkled. Instead of the dark wood tones and serious-faced portraits of Pendulum House, the academy was bright with feminine colors, lavender walls with white borders, and scenic paintings of flowery hillsides and brightly lit ponds.

The air smelled faintly of flowers, and the sound of a piano drifted through one of the open doors down the hall. It was Oona's first time in the highly prestigious boarding school, and as she followed Madame Iree up the curving staircase, she couldn't help but feel a twinge of unease. It wasn't just that she felt out of place—which she did, but that was okay because that was a feeling

Oona had gotten used to long ago—but it was because when Oona had been younger, before her parents had died, her mother had encouraged her to attend the academy. Her mother had been a member, and it had seemed only fitting that her daughter should follow in her footsteps—that was, until Oona's uncle chose her as his apprentice.

Oona's mother had let go of the idea, but Oona had always harbored a sense of guilt that she hadn't fulfilled her mother's wishes. And then of course there was the thought that if she had attended the academy, instead of accepting the apprenticeship and learning magic, then her mother and her sister might still be alive. She remembered what Madame Romania from Romania had hinted at, that Oona might be innocent of the tragedy after all. But there was only one way to know for sure, which made discovering the punchbowl's location imperative.

As Oona and Madame Iree ascended the stairs, they came upon several younger girls being mentored by older girls on the proper way to walk up and down a flight of stairs. The younger girls had broomsticks tied to their backs to keep them straight. Oona thought it almost comical as she listened to one of the older girls giving precise instructions on how high to lift the hem of the skirt without the fear of being scandalized, or tripping on one's own dress.

The young lady giving the lesson—a tall schoolgirl with fiery red hair and a mouth that reminded Oona of a lizard—glanced Oona over from head to foot, and then snickered. She pointed at Oona's feet, as if making fun of the way she was walking. Oona looked away as the girls all began to giggle, choosing to ignore them. Oona's mother had taught her to walk properly—*without the need of broomsticks, thank you very much*—and in that moment she decided that she was all the better for never having attended such a ridiculous school.

Isadora's room was the first at the top of the stairs. To Oona's astonishment, Madame Iree didn't bother to knock, but flung the door open and glided gracefully in as if it were her own private suite.

"Isadora, dear," said Madame Iree, "you have guests."

"Mother!" Isadora shouted, clearly surprised.

Oona stepped into the room, catching a whiff of some mighty strong perfume. Isadora, who was sitting on her bed, quickly shoved something beneath her pillow. Madame Iree seemed not to have noticed.

"You know Miss Crate, Isadora?" she said, extending her hand. "She says she has something of yours."

Oona's gaze darted around the room, looking for any sign of the punchbowl. Madame Romania from Romania had said it was precisely thirteen inches in diameter and made of finely etched crystal. Oona saw nothing of the sort, not on the dressing table, nor the bedside table, nor the dresser.

A double wardrobe stood open, revealing countless dresses packed so tightly that Oona was quite certain not one more single dress, let alone a thirteen-inch punch-bowl, could fit inside. Below the dresses, at the bottom of the cabinet, she could see Isadora's shoes lined up in perfectly even rows—again no sign of the missing bowl.

Oona was curious, however, as to what Isadora was hiding beneath her pillow.

Isadora glanced at Oona, managing to look both surprised and smug at the same time. "You have something of mine?" she asked. "Whatever could it be?"

Oona reached into her pocket and brought out the ring. She held it between her thumb and forefinger.

Isadora's eyebrows came together, a puzzled look on her face. It was not the reaction Oona was expecting. To her surprise, it was Madame Iree who reacted.

"Oh, my dear, where did you find it?" she asked. "I've been wondering what happened to my ring since the party last night."

"It's yours?" asked both Oona and Isadora at the same time.

Madame Iree's face went red. She opened her mouth, as if to explain, but then her lips suddenly clamped shut, and she held out her hand. "Thank you for returning my ring, Miss Crate. It no doubt slipped from my finger when the architect knocked me over and spilled his soup on my dress. Highly embarrassing."

Oona's eyebrows rose. "No doubt," she said, doing her best to conceal her disbelief. The ring had of course been found beneath the caravan, nowhere near the site of the soup-spilling incident, and Oona had a feeling that Madame Iree was not telling the whole story. Regardless, she placed the ring in the dressmaker's open palm.

Madame Iree turned abruptly to her daughter and asked: "Isadora, what have you got hidden beneath your pillow?"

Oona wondered briefly if Madame Iree's sudden interest in what Isadora was concealing was simply a convenient way to divert attention away from herself and the ring. If that was the case, then it was a good ploy. Oona's heart leapt. Could it be this easy? Was Isadora's theft about to be revealed?

Isadora's eyes shifted nervously, glancing from Oona to Madame Iree.

"N-n-nothing," Isadora stuttered.

"Come, come, Isadora. I saw you shift something beneath your pillow when I came in," her mother insisted.

Isadora's eyes narrowed. "*Barged* in would be more appropriate. Have you ever heard of knocking, Mother?"

Madame Iree ignored the sarcasm. "What are you hiding, Isadora? Show me this instant."

Isadora licked her lips, and then pulled a letter from beneath the pillow. "It is a . . . a . . . a poem. From my BOYFRIEND!"

"Oh," said Madame Iree. "Is that all? Why were you hiding it?"

"Because," Isadora said indignantly. "It is a private matter, and . . . we're not supposed to have letters from boys in our rooms. Academy rules. Anyway, Roderick doesn't . . . um . . . well, he does not wish for others to know he is a poet. He's afraid they will think him unmanly."

"That's ridiculous," said Madame Iree, and Oona had to agree. For a boy so concerned with being chivalrous, she thought it silly for Roderick to worry about what others thought of his poetry. Madame Iree wandered to the dressing table, where she picked up the blue ribbon Isadora had won earlier that day. "Have you figured out your clue yet, Miss Crate?"

The question took Oona by surprise, and she couldn't help but feel a hint of challenge in it. Perhaps even a taunt.

Like mother like daughter, Oona thought before saying: "I . . . um . . . am working on it."

Madame Iree nodded confidently and glanced at Isadora. The two of them grinned at each other, as if they held a great secret.

109

"And you, Isadora?" Oona found herself asking, and hating herself for giving in to the trap. "How are you doing with the clue?"

Isadora sank back into her pillow and waggled her eyebrows. "Figured it out hours ago. Really, I'm surprised you haven't gotten it yet." She feigned a yawn, and then snapped her fingers. "Easy as one . . . two . . . three."

Madame Iree clapped her hands together. "That's my girl. Smart as a whip."

Oona knew that if Deacon had been there, he would have been helpless to correct Madame Iree, explaining that the saying was actually "*quick* as a whip." She suddenly wished for his company.

It was only moments later that she had reason to wish for his company a second time, though this time for protection rather than grammatical advice.

"Look at the hem of that dress!" said a sharp, foreboding voice from behind Oona.

She turned to find Headmistress Duvet looming in the doorway. Her glass eye gave the impression that it was looking sideways at her good eye: the good eye that presently leered menacingly at Oona's feet.

Oona looked down for the first time that evening and could see where the hem of her dress had been burned in the ape house challenge, and it became painfully obvious what the girls on the stairs had been laughing at. She had been so preoccupied with losing to Isadora—not to mention the mystery of the missing punchbowl—that she'd neglected to change her dress. Oona's white, stocking-clad ankles showed beneath the dark burned fabric, and the dress appeared several inches shorter than when she had first put it on that morning.

"Oh," she said, examining her ankle. "That's . . . um . . . well . . . that's—"

"Highly improper!" said Headmistress Duvet, her good eye all at once gleaming even brighter than her glass one, and it wasn't until it was too late that Oona noticed the cane from the entryway in the woman's hand. The headmistress raised it up, the word IMPROPER printed on the paddle as large as a newspaper headline, and Oona closed her eyes in anticipation of impact.

CHAPTER SEVEN

The Silk

"S he actually swatted you?" Deacon perched himself atop the mirror, sounding aghast.

Oona eased herself onto the chair in front of her dressing table, a bag of never-melting ice beneath her aching bum.

"She did indeed," she said, "and I can't believe you let me go out dressed like that. Either of you."

Samuligan stood attentively near the door, his crescent grin just visible beneath the shadow of his cowboy hat. "I thought it rather becoming. Though, admittedly, ahead of its time. Just wait, three months from now, all the girls will be burning the hems of their skirts, and the dress shops of Dark Street will reek of smoke from the Glass Gates all the way to New York City."

"Very funny," Oona said, looking herself over in the mirror. "A real trendsetter."

She took in the reflection of her room, which she decided would never have passed the inspection of Headmistress Duvet's severe scrutiny. Glass vials and laboratory beakers lay messily across the dressing table, along with various untidy piles of paper.

She pulled the ribbon containing the contest clue from her pocket, and mimicked Isadora's smug tone. "Easy as one, two, three!" She tossed the ribbon to the table. "So now it seems that Madame Iree is the most likely suspect for the punchbowl thief."

"How so?" Deacon asked.

"Well, as I told you on the ride home, it was not Isadora's ring that you found beneath the caravan's trap-door after all. It was her mother's."

"But you said Madame Iree claims to have lost the ring when she and the architect fell to the ground during the soup-spilling incident at the party," Deacon reasoned.

"And what then?" Oona asked. "The ring just got up and walked beneath the caravan on its own?"

"Perhaps it's an enchanted ring," Samuligan suggested.

"That is always a possibility," Oona admitted. "But that still gives no explanation as to why it fell from her hand in front of the stage, and then ended up beneath the caravan. Unless, of course, she is lying. It could be that she ran into the architect on purpose."

"Why would she do that?" Deacon asked.

"Well, consider this possibility," Oona said. "Madame Iree crawls beneath the caravan in order to sneak inside and steal the punchbowl. The ring slips from her finger, and she gets mud all over her dress. After stealing the punch-bowl, she then returns to the party and collides with the architect. The soup spills on her dress, and the two of them fall to the ground. Madame Iree uses this as an excuse to return home to change her sullied dress. She then uses the punchbowl to give Isadora the answers to the clues."

"But where does she hide the punchbowl?" Deacon asked. "Before she leaves the party, how dose she smuggle it out of the park without anyone seeing?"

"Good question," Oona said. "Perhaps . . . she has it beneath her dress?"

Samuligan threw back his head and howled with laughter, causing Oona's mirror to crack down the middle. Deacon leapt from the mirror, shrieking in surprise before settling on the bedpost.

"Samuligan!" Oona said. "Look what you've done."

The faerie servant cleared his throat. "Forgive me," he said, and then spit onto his finger. The saliva blobbed at the end of his long, bony fingertip, which he used to run down the crack in the mirror. When he was done, the crack had disappeared and the glass appeared as good as new.

"Well, you just saved yourself seven years bad luck," Oona said.

"Only seven?" Samuligan said. "That's nothing. I once had a cousin in Faerie who had a three-hundred-year stretch of bad luck."

Oona smiled. It wasn't often that Samuligan spoke of his life before Pendulum House. It intrigued her. However, she did not wish to get sidetracked.

"Well," she said, "what do you think of my theory of Madame Iree?"

"Rather dreary," said Samuligan.

Deacon fluttered his wings irritably. "Don't you think you should put your full concentration into figuring out that clue?" He pointed his beak at the ribbon on the table. "Or are you already forgetting what happened earlier today when you dillydallied?"

Oona sighed, shifting in her seat. Her backside suddenly stung from where Headmistress Duvet's paddle had smacked home. She picked up the ribbon. "Deacon is right. Let's get to the bottom of this, right now."

By the following morning, however, Oona was no closer to solving the clue than when she'd first received it. The memory of Isadora's voice continued to pester her: "Easy as one, two, three."

Oona's eyes were so dry and red that they felt as if they might catch fire. More than half the night she'd spent lying awake in bed, and yet it had not been the clue on the ribbon that had kept her from sleep so much as the problem of the missing punchbowl.

At the breakfast table, she found her uncle hurriedly stuffing a biscuit into his mouth and looking highly agitated.

"I'm afraid I'm going to need your assistance," the Wizard said. "I know you have the contest to think about, but there has been another incident concerning the throttler's silk problem in the garment district." He held up a note with charred edges, indicating that he had been sent a note via flame. "I just received word that a swath of the faerie fabric has come to life and tied itself around a merchant and his wife. It is refusing to let them go. I know that I relieved you of your apprentice duties during the contest, but this silk business has gotten dreadfully out of control."

Oona looked forlornly at the clue in her hand and sighed. "Of course, Uncle. But the contest starts at noon, and I still haven't figured out this clue."

The Wizard glanced at the clock over the door. "It is eight o'clock now. That should leave plenty of time. Samuligan, ready the carriage."

Samuligan snapped his fingers, silvery sparks shooting from their tips. He spun dramatically around and then disappeared through the servant's entrance on his way to the stable.

Wonderful, Oona thought gloomily. *Just what I need: more distractions.*

It was a selfish thought, she knew. Her uncle would not have asked for her help unless he truly needed it, and it sounded as if this enchanted silk might be quite dangerous. Helping the merchant and his wife was surely more urgent than solving the contest clue, yet Oona began to wonder if she would ever have time to figure it out.

It's my own fault for not spending more time on it yesterday, she thought reproachfully, and then quickly grabbed a muffin before heading out the front door.

Several minutes later she climbed into the carriage beside her uncle, unable to escape the nagging thought that Isadora already had the answer to the clue, and that she had learned the answer from the stolen punchbowl. There was simply no other explanation.

The carriage clacked over the cobbled street, taking them past Oswald Park and then the shopping district, where candlestick trees lined the sidewalks glowing faintly in the morning mist. A large sign outside the Dark Street theater read:

BE AMAZED! BRING YOUR FRIENDS!

ALBERT PANCAKE

IS

THE MASTER OF TEN THOUSAND FACES

ONE WEEK ONLY

TICKETS GOING FAST!

GET YOURS AT THE BOX OFFICE TODAY!!!

"Look, Oona," the Wizard said. "A new show. Looks fascinating."

"Hmm?" she intoned, looking vaguely at the sign. "Oh, yes, I suppose. But tell me, Uncle, why do you think all of this throttler's silk is showing up? Where is it coming from?"

"That is just the thing," the Wizard replied. "There is only one place it *could* come from."

"Faerie," Oona said, and suddenly her stomach felt as if it had been twisted into a tight knot. "And there is only one person I can think of who knows how to get through the Glass Gates."

Deacon shook his head grimly on her shoulder. "Red Martin."

Oona and the Wizard nodded in agreement, and the three of them fell decidedly quiet for the remainder of the trip. It wasn't until Samuligan pulled the carriage to the side of the road that the Wizard broke the silence.

"Oh, dear, this is no good at all!" he exclaimed, throwing open the compartment door and leaping to the curb. It took Oona a moment to realize what had gotten him so excited.

Through the window she could make out what appeared to be a man and a woman tied to a lamppost outside a fabric store. What was even more peculiar was how the bloodred fabric that kept them in place appeared to be slithering out of the store and wrapping itself around the couple much like a giant serpent.

"Quickly, Oona, Samuligan!" the Wizard barked at them as he raced to the victims' aid.

"Oh, my," Deacon said as Oona hopped to the sidewalk and started after her uncle. Samuligan was close behind.

A cluster of horrified spectators stood nearby, all shaking their heads and pointing at the bizarre scene, and as Oona neared the trapped couple, she could make out the terrified expressions on their faces, both of which were beginning to turn blue. The silk was strangling them, and Oona realized that there was no time to waste.

"What do we do?" she asked, feeling frantic. This was the first time since her encounter with the stolen mind daggers that she had come upon such a deadly mystical object, and presently she went blank as to what needed to happen.

Luckily the Wizard was there to take charge. He drew

a wooden wand from his robe, aimed it at the silk snaking out of the store across the sidewalk, and shouted: *"Dimittere!"*

This, Oona knew, was the spell used to release one thing from another, such as an apple from a tree, but the spell did not seem to have the same effect on the silk. A jet of white light shot from the tip of the Wizard's wand and collided with the cloth in a burst of sparks. But instead of releasing the victims from the silk's constricting grip, the spell only made the enchanted material more ferocious than ever.

The free end of the fabric suddenly slithered out of the store like an eel and attempted to wrap itself around the Wizard's foot. He leapt back just in time, but before he could jump again, the silk darted up and snatched his wand from his hand. It smacked him in the head with it several times and then tossed it across the street.

"Well, that was certainly rude," the Wizard said.

The fabric reared back and spread open, taking on the shape of an enormous red cobra preparing to strike. Oona's heart dropped. She still did not know what to do. But in the next instant Samuligan leapt between the Wizard and the striking fabric.

The silk threw itself at the faerie, its bloodred surface rippling like a storm-battered flag, and suddenly the two of them, the faerie and the fabric, were locked together in a brutal wrestling match on the sidewalk. At first it seemed that Samuligan was getting the best of the murderous material, but then just as quickly the game changed and the silk managed to wrap itself around the faerie's neck and mouth, preventing him from uttering a spell.

Like the other witnesses, Oona was terrified. Samuligan the Fay was the most powerful magical being she had ever encountered. If this throttler's silk was able to overpower him, she hadn't a clue how she and her uncle were supposed to stop it.

"Oona," the Wizard shouted at her as he rushed across the street to retrieve his wand. "Try *Duratus frigidam*!"

Oona jumped in surprise. *Duratus frigidam* was a freezing spell, one that she had not practiced in over three years. It took superb concentration, even with her extraordinary natural powers, and she wondered briefly if she was up to the task. What if something went wrong? Would it be her fault that these people died? And what about Samuligan?

Unfortunately, there was no time to waver. Oona raised her hands dramatically above her head, preparing to cast the spell, but the Wizard called to her from across the street: "You'll need a directional conductor!"

The words to the spell halted on her lips and her heart skipped a beat as she realized how closely she had just come to causing another tragedy.

Of course, she chided herself. *Duratus frigidam requires a directional conductor,* which she knew was merely a fancy way of saying: a wand, or a staff, or something to channel the spell in a specific direction.

Without a wand it was possible she might freeze not only the fabric, but also Samuligan and the man and woman tied to the lamppost, not to mention the bystanders and possibly even herself. Such was the nature of conductor spells.

Oona did not own a wand, however, but being a Natural Magician certainly had its advantages. Three months ago she had conducted the Lights of Wonder spell through a broken chair leg. Most any narrow object would do, and presently Oona reached into a dress pocket and removed her father's magnifying glass. Quieting her mind as best she could, she aimed the wooden handle at the fabric on the sidewalk.

"Duratus frigidam!" she cried, and all at once her head felt as if it had just been plunged into a tub of ice-cold water.

Deacon shot from her shoulder as if he had been stung by a bee. Oona clinched her teeth against the discomfort as a steady stream of dartlike snowflakes shot from the end of the handle and began attaching themselves to the middle of the silk.

Instantly, the flakes began to multiply across the

material, extending in both directions. The fabric began to freeze solid.

"*Duratus frigidam!*" the Wizard shouted, and Oona saw that her uncle stood beside her, wand in hand, and was adding his own spell to hers. It occurred to her then that perhaps her uncle was not such a mediocre magician after all, despite what everyone seemed to think.

The freezing process quickened, and a moment later Samuligan tore free of the silk's grip, causing the entire strip of fabric to shatter like glass. Oona and the Wizard simultaneously released their spells as the man and woman toppled from the lamppost to the sidewalk, gasping desperately for breath.

"Well, now," said the Wizard. "That seems to have done the trick."

Deacon returned to Oona's shoulder as she slowly let out her breath and her head returned to its normal temperature. Tattered bits of frozen red cloth blew about in the breeze as the Wizard approached the man and woman.

"Are you quite all right?" he asked, extending a hand to help the woman to her feet.

"I . . . I think so," she said. She threw a chilling glance toward the man, whom Samuligan was helping to stand up straight.

Unlike the disheveled appearance of the man and woman, Oona noted, Samuligan did not appear any the worse for wear from his tussle with the deadly cloth, not so much as a wrinkled jacket or a fold in his cowboy hat.

The woman continued to stare coldly at the man. "I would be much better if my husband here could manage to stay away from the Nightshade Casino."

"I told you, dear," the man replied, rubbing at his neck, "I stopped going several weeks ago."

The woman folded her arms and tutted. "Yes, but not before you went into so much debt you couldn't repay it all."

"Oh, dear," said the Wizard. He looked understandingly at the man. "You are indebted to Red Martin?"

The man nodded and bowed his head. Oona could tell he felt ashamed of himself, and it seemed equally clear that the Wizard was sympathetic to his situation. The Wizard had unknowingly found himself in debt to Red Martin's Nightshade Corporation, having been duped by his scoundrel of a lawyer, Mr. Ravensmith, and was still trying to get out of the financial mess.

The wife did not appear so sympathetic. She narrowed her eyes at her husband, and said: "Of course it's Red Martin behind this. Who else could it be?"

The Wizard glanced at the storefront. "Is this your fabric shop?"

"It is," said the woman. She pointed to the sign, which read: DODGER FABRICS. "I am Mrs. Elizabeth Dodger, and this is my husband, Orris." Mrs. Dodger's temper all at once melted, and she threw her arms around the Wizard. "We are so grateful you came along. Oh, thank you, thank you!"

The woman released the Wizard and then threw herself at Oona, wrapping her in her arms. Oona could not help but feel slightly uncomfortable as the woman began to sob into her shoulder. Unable to think of anything else to do, Oona patted her gingerly on the back.

At last Mrs. Dodger pulled away, and as she turned back to the Wizard, Samuligan opened his arms wide, displaying his frighteningly wide grin with too many teeth, as if anticipating his own hug. Mrs. Dodger hesitated briefly—Oona thought she saw the woman shiver slightly—and then acted as if the faerie servant was not there.

For an instant Oona felt bad for Samuligan, but then he gave her a wink, and she realized that he had only been playing with the woman. It would, of course, have been unfitting for the lady to be seen hugging a servant, which Oona felt was simply ridiculous, considering that Samuligan had been trying to save the woman's life. But still, that was the way things were, and people rarely went against such social rules.

Mr. Dodger cleared his throat. "We received the silk with a new shipment today. Someone must have placed it in with the other fabrics, because we certainly did not order any red silk."

The Wizard nodded, his aged eyes looking concerned. "If you have read the paper, then you will know that you are not the only ones who have received the silk. We'll need to do a search of the premises to make sure there isn't any more."

Both Mr. and Mrs. Dodger's eyebrows shot up, and the two of them looked jerkily around in alarm. Despite her angry words toward her husband, Mrs. Dodger clutched nervously at Mr. Dodger's arm.

"But if you will excuse me a moment," the Wizard added, "I would like a minute with my apprentice." He led Oona toward the carriage, leaving the anxious-looking Dodgers clutching at each other in front of the store. The Wizard beamed. "That was incredible control you showed back there, Oona dear."

Oona allowed herself a smile. "I did manage it all right, didn't I?"

"You did indeed. And for that, I couldn't be prouder," he said.

"I almost forgot the conductor, though," she admitted, still feeling guilty for having almost cast *Duratus frigidam* freehanded.

Certain spells required a conductor while others did not. It was important, she knew, to know which was which. *Ignigtis,* the illusory fireball, was an example of a nonconductor spell, as well as *Reconcilio,* which she had once used to repair her father's broken magnifying glass. Even the extraordinary *Switch* enchantment she had used on Red Martin beneath Witch Hill was magic she could perform without wand work—but spells such as *Lux lucis admiratio* and *Duratus frigidam* demanded the accuracy of a conductor. She knew all too well that she needed to be careful. Unlike faeries, who were so in tune with their magic that they could control its direction with nothing more than their thoughts, the human body was nowhere near as accurate.

The Wizard raised one bushy white eyebrow. "Yes, you *almost* forgot, but in the end, you did it right. That is the main thing, and you should be proud of yourself."

"Yes, indeed," Deacon added from her shoulder. "It was most impressive."

Oona's smile widened.

The Wizard clapped his hands together. "Now, I think it is time you got back to your contest. Samuligan can take you to the park. Meanwhile, I'll have a look through the rest of the Dodgers' inventory to make sure there isn't any more of the silk lurking around."

"Are you sure you'll be all right on your own?" Oona asked.

He nodded assuredly. "Now that I know the proper

spell to use the first time, I'm sure I'll manage just fine. If there is time, I will take a hansom cab to the park, though I have a feeling this may take quite a while. I must be thorough."

"Of course, Uncle. Just . . . please be careful," she said, and though she did not consider herself to be the affectionate type, she gave in to the impulse and gave him a fervent hug. Deacon cawed uncomfortably from her shoulder as the Wizard patted her on the back.

As Oona turned to go, the Wizard stopped her.

"And one more thing, Oona dear," he said with a glow about his eyes.

"What's that, Uncle?" she asked.

He gave her a wink. "Good luck."

CHAPTER EIGHT

The Ribbon Clue

Dark Street slid past the carriage windows, its crooked structures like shadowy, misshapen figures crammed shoulder to shoulder in too tight of a space. The upper stories of the buildings leaned dizzily over the sidewalks and against one another, their oddly shaped windows staring down on the bustle about town.

Horse-drawn carriages clacked over damp morning cobblestones, and pedestrians buzzed busily about the sidewalks: the ladies in their high-bustled dresses, the men in jackets and bowler hats. It was the everyday activity of a modern city.

There was nothing to suggest that the citizens lived any differently from residents of London, England—the street was sometimes called Little London Town, after all—and yet, people aside, one could not travel far on Dark Street before coming across some peculiarity or another. Sometimes subtle (a window with no reflection, or a water fountain that ran in reverse) and sometimes not so subtle (an enchanted cello that played on its own, or the passing shadow of a nonexistent dragon), the oddities were a constant reminder of the street's deep roots in magic.

A puzzling thought occurred to Oona as the carriage clattered north toward the park, and she couldn't help but wonder why she had not considered it before now. The incident with the throttler's silk was all at once obliterated from her mind as she sat forward in her seat, finger pressing ponderously against her lips.

"There's something that I don't understand, Deacon," she said. "Why would Madame Iree favor her daughter to win over her son?"

Deacon stood on the seat opposite her and cocked his head. "What do you mean?"

"I mean, why would she steal the punchbowl and use it to give Isadora the answers to the clues, and not share them with her son, Adler, as well?"

"That is a very good question," Deacon replied. "And an even better question would be: Why on earth would you concern yourself with that now, when we are presently on our way to the second set of challenges, and you still haven't figured out that clue?"

A line creased Oona's forehead. She looked at the ribbon, running her thumb over the silky surface, and feeling as if her head might burst.

Go see the RAIN AIR EVENT
Ask for the PRICE ON UP
Take it to the STREAM of SNOT HAUNTED Faces
At the Dark EARTH TREE TEST

It was strange. Never before had she felt so confused about a clue. No doubt it had something to do with the fact that each time she focused on the words, more questions slipped into her mind regarding the punchbowl theft. Where was it now? Perhaps in the back of Madame Iree's dress shop. Or was there something more sinister at play? After all, if the bowl could actually answer any question, then just about anyone would have a motive for wanting to take it. Even Red Martin himself, should he come to know about it, would stop at nothing to get his hands on such a powerful tool.

And what about—

But Oona's thoughts came to an abrupt halt along with the carriage. She went forward and then back, slamming down hard on her seat.

"Ouch, that hurt!" she cried.

Samuligan had brought the carriage to a surprising

stop in the middle of the street, and Oona could hear shouts of irritation from the carriage drivers behind them. Sticking her head out the open window, Oona glanced back, seeing a line of carriages suddenly backed up behind them, each of the drivers either shouting their displeasure, or shaking their fists in the air.

Turning forward, Oona saw why Samuligan had reined in the horse. She laughed. Less than a foot in front of the horse, she could see a line of multicolored beetles crossing the street. The average human driver would have missed seeing them altogether, Oona knew, or even if they had seen them, they would most likely have ridden right over the beautiful insects. But Samuligan was certainly not human, and it was a testament to his unpredictable faerie nature that he would hold up traffic on a busy morning to allow the insects to cross the street unharmed.

Three voices struck up a cord, humming in perfect harmony, before launching into a grim ballad of love lost.

Glancing out the other side of the carriage, Oona saw that the voices were coming from the three-headed sing-ing lamppost, which, up until three weeks ago, had been a permanent fixture in the Dark Street restaurant dis-trict. Apparently, the restaurant owners had finally had enough of what they called "the obnoxious lamp" and commissioned the Wizard to move it to another location.

The Wizard had agreed, and now the magical lamppost resided beside the joke-telling clock in front of the Dark Street Theater, where it sang songs of tragic love upon each hour.

"Woe, woe, woe is me.
Adrift and alone on a tear-filled sea.
Sad, bewildered, misunderstood,
My one true love is gone for good.
How my heart does shrink and ache
And never again will I eat cake
Since she left with the baker's son
And now I'm stuck without no fun."

Deacon shuttered at the incorrectness of the final sentence, puffing up his chest for what was sure to be an impassioned lesson on the improper use of the English language, but Oona held her hand up, her gaze fixed out the window.

Deacon squawked, as if the effort to hold back his lesson had been a great one, and then asked: "What is it?"

"Look," Oona said, and pointed at the sign outside the theater. "Do you see it, Deacon?"

Deacon hopped to the other end of the passenger compartment and nodded. "Yes, your uncle spoke of it on the way to the garment district."

Oona vaguely remembered her uncle pointing it out. She had been so caught up in her own thoughts that she had not been very interested, but now that she looked at it properly she realized that the sign was of the utmost importance.

She read aloud:

"BE AMAZED! BRING YOUR FRIENDS!
ALBERT PANCAKE

IS

THE MASTER OF TEN THOUSAND FACES

ONE WEEK ONLY

TICKETS GOING FAST!

GET YOURS AT THE BOX OFFICE TODAY!!!"

Two artistic sketches, one on either side of the text, depicted the images of two famous people from the World of Man: Abraham Lincoln and Cleopatra. Oona knew their faces from her history lessons with Deacon, but it was not the images that caught her attention.

"Yes, I see it," Deacon said, sounding unimpressed. "It appears to be some sort of quick-change/one-man impersonator show. Not my sort of thing, really. I prefer the classics: Shakespeare and the like."

Oona smiled, and her heart began to work faster. The carriage moved forward as she held the clue up to the light and read out loud: "Take it to the STREAM of SNOT HAUNTED Faces."

When Deacon did not immediately respond, she pointed to the theater sign, and then turned the ribbon toward Deacon. "Don't you see? The letters are all mixed up. Look at the words printed in all capital letters in the clue. Why didn't I see it before? They are anagrams." Again she pointed to the receding theater sign. "See the word MASTER?"

Deacon took in a sharp breath: "It has the same letters as the word stream."

"Indeed, Deacon. STREAM is an anagram for MASTER. And mix up the letters in SNOT HAUNTED and you get . . ."

Deacon nodded before leaping enthusiastically to her shoulder. "TEN THOUSAND!"

Oona pulled the ribbon taut. "So that line of the clue should read: 'Take it to the Master of Ten Thousand Faces.'"

"Take what?" Deacon asked.

"Excellent question," Oona said. "But first, look at the last line. It makes sense now."

"At the Dark EARTH TREE TEST?" Deacon said questioningly. "I've never heard of such a thing."

"But again," Oona said excitedly, "the letters printed in capitals are anagrams. Once you know what to look for, it's hard not to see it."

Deacon stared at the ribbon, but could not make it out.

"I'll give you a hint," Oona said. "Where is the Master of Ten Thousand Faces performing?"

"At the . . ." He trailed off, suddenly seeing it for himself. "*EARTH TREE TEST* is an anagram for *STREET THEATER.*"

"Correct," Oona said. She could feel her mind really beginning to move now, smooth and focused, taking its footing on the solid foundation of logic and reason. She felt invigorated. "Take it to the Master of Ten Thousand Faces, at the Dark Street Theater," she said. "So apparently we are supposed to bring something to Albert Pancake, who is the Master of Ten Thousand Faces at the Dark Street Theater."

"Again, what are we supposed to bring?" Deacon asked.

Oona glanced at the first line "Go see the RAIN AIR EVENT," and then focused her attention out the window. She scratched at her chin, watching the street vendors hustle about the outdoor market, but she did not really see them. The letters of the clue danced in her mind's eye, rearranging themselves like pickup sticks.

Indeed, Oona was so preoccupied that she nearly missed seeing Isadora Iree exit the veterinarian's office with a box tucked under her arm.

"Look, Deacon. It's Isadora," Oona said, quite surprised. "Where is she going? The park is in the other direction."

"Perhaps she's given up," Deacon said. He hopped to the windowsill and watched Isadora walk hurriedly away.

"Unlikely," Oona said. "She's up to something. What was that she had under her arm?"

"In the box?" Deacon said. "You aren't suggesting that it is this mysterious punchbowl, are you?"

Oona squinted out the window at Isadora's shrinking form. "It is just about the right size."

"She was coming out of the veterinarian's office," Deacon said. "Perhaps it is a sick pet."

Oona felt a jolt of energy shoot through her like a bolt of lighting. She sat forward in her seat. "Repeat that, Deacon."

"I said, perhaps it is a sick pet."

"No. The first part. You said she was coming out of the . . ." Oona trailed off, attempting to spell out the letters in her head.

"Veterinarian's office," Deacon finished for her.

Oona bounced her fist against the carriage door. "And *VETERINARIAN* is an anagram for *RAIN AIR EVENT*."

Deacon was silent as he did the calculation in his head. A moment later he began to flap his wings in excitement.

"By Oswald, you're right! So the clue should read 'Go see the veterinarian."

"Which means," Oona said, "that Isadora has taken the lead once again. Samuligan!" She banged several times on the roof. "Turn this horse cart around at once! We're off to see the veterinarian!"

CHAPTER NINE

The Master of Ten Thousand Faces

T he bell over the door tinkled as Oona stepped into the front room of the Dark Street Veterinarian's Office. Deacon's talons tightened on Oona's shoulder, and she could tell he was nervous about entering the animal doctor's office.

The room smelled of dog breath and cat dander. Several owners sat in chairs along the wall, their ailing pets either lying in their laps or resting at their heels. Upon seeing Deacon, a fat orange-and-white tabby cat let out a low growl, but was too weak to do more than rear its head from its owner's lap, a middle-aged woman with cat fur clinging to the front of her dress.

The office was more of an apartment than any office

Oona had ever been in, and several seconds after she'd entered the front room, a man with a drooping mustache and a reflector strapped to his forehead poked his face through the doorway leading to the kitchen area. Below the reflector, several long needlelike objects stuck straight out of the man's creased forehead. Several more needles poked out of his chin like long, extremely rigid whiskers. The needles looked very painful, and Oona had no idea what to make of them.

"Do you have an appointment?" the man shouted hurriedly.

When Oona hesitated, he stuck out his left hand, plucked several needles from his palm, and then snapped his fingers impatiently. "Come, come! Plenty of sick pets here, and I have nine house calls scheduled for this afternoon."

"Oh, yes," said Oona. "I mean, no. I haven't an appointment. Are you the veterinarian?"

"Of course I'm the veterinarian!" the man shouted. He stepped fully into the doorway, displaying his long white doctor's jacket. He held up his right hand, which was also stuck with dozens of the strange needles. "Why else would I be performing massage therapy on porcupines?"

"I . . . can't imagine," Oona replied.

"Highly anxious creatures, porcupines," said the veterinarian. "Carry all of their stress in their backs."

A hound let out a low whimper, and its owner, a boy of ten or eleven, patted the dog sympathetically on the head. Oona suddenly wished to be far away.

"Indeed," she said. "Well, I don't want to waste your valuable time. I've come for the *'rope in cup.'*"

"The what?" shouted the veterinarian.

Oona ran the anagram over in her mind: *Ask for the PRICE ON UP.* "The . . . ah . . . 'rope in cup'?" she asked, questioningly.

The veterinarian plucked one of the porcupine needles from his chin, pointing it at her. "I haven't any idea what you are talking about. There is no rope in cup here, and if you insist on blabbering nonsense, then I will have to ask you to leave. These porcupines aren't going to massage themselves."

Oona shook her head. She had not been a hundred percent sure of her attempt to decipher the anagram, but it had been the only solution she could come up with for PRICE ON UP.

She glanced quickly around the room. According to the clue, she was supposed to come here and ask for something, but what? What was another anagram for PRICE ON UP? Seeing the sad-eyed puppy in the lap of a sleeping elderly gentleman—both the puppy and the man had drool running down their mouths—Oona quickly said: "Pup on rice!"

The veterinarian looked as if he were about to throw the porcupine barb at Oona. "I'm sure I have no idea what you are speaking of!" he shouted. "Now, unless you are here to take one of these anxiety-ridden porcupines off my hands, then please find your way to the door."

"Wait!" Oona shouted back at him. "Porcupine!"

"Yes, that's what I said," the veterinarian said. "No doubt their anxiety is from all that show business the owner's got them involved in. Highly stressful work for an animal."

"That's it!" Oona exclaimed, seeing the letters in PRICE ON UP rearrange themselves in her head to form the word: "Porcupine! I've come to take a porcupine to the Master of Ten Thousand Faces at the Dark Street Theater."

"That's what that other girl asked for straightaway," said the woman with the orange tabby cat on her lap.

"Isadora Iree?" Oona asked.

The woman only shrugged, but Oona was sure it was Isadora whom the woman was referring to: Isadora, who somehow had figured everything out well ahead of Oona, and was most likely at the Dark Street Theater at that very minute, handing her porcupine to Albert Pancake.

"Good riddance!" shouted the veterinarian. He handed a box containing one of the porcupines to Oona. As she turned to leave, Roderick Rutherford opened the door and stepped into the front room. The first thing Oona noticed was the bruise below his left eye.

"Ah, Miss Crate," he said. "One step ahead of me, as usual."

"Only barely, it seems," she replied. "And Isadora is ahead of us both."

Roderick nodded, then pointed at the box in her hands. "That must be your porcupine."

Oona shook her head. "Am I the only one who had such trouble figuring that one out?"

Roderick smirked, then winced at the pain in his cheek. Oona opened her mouth to ask Roderick what had happened to his face, when she suddenly realized that not only was he about to get his own porcupine, but Isadora had quite a large lead already. She decided to save the question for another time.

"Good luck, Mr. Rutherford," she said. "But I really must run."

Oona flung open the carriage door and made a dash for the Dark Street Theater box office window, the box containing the porcupine clasped beneath her arm. She skidded to a halt and Deacon flew to her shoulder.

"I'm here to see the Master of Ten Thousand Faces,"

she said, peering through the glass. "I have a porcupine to deliver."

The woman behind the glass did not bother to look up from her newspaper, but pointed to the front doors.

"Thank you," Oona said.

A carriage clattered to a stop behind her on the street, and Oona saw that Roderick was right behind her, carrying the box containing his own porcupine. She pushed open the front door, and Roderick followed her in. Pausing for a moment to let her eyes adjust to the darkened theater lobby, Oona took in her surroundings. Roderick did the same.

A lush red-and-gold carpet spread out beneath their feet, running from wall to wall and continuing up the twin staircases that curved up to the mezzanine on the second floor. A line of marble columns supported the mezzanine from below, each column carved to resemble enormous twisted tree trunks. It was like finding oneself in a marble forest. The high ceiling supported no less than five brilliant crystal chandeliers that glimmered and sparkled like diamonds in the sky.

But all of this opulence and grandeur failed to catch Oona's interest. It was the dragon that stood in the center of the room that took hold of her attention and refused to let go.

Oona's heart lurched. She took a step back as the beast

first reared its head, and then turned to face her. Deacon let out a sharp shriek before launching himself into the air and taking refuge on one of the chandeliers high overhead. Roderick leapt behind Oona, as if to use her as a shield, and Oona thought: *He wouldn't know what chivalry was if it hit him over the head.*

The Dragon stepped forward. Oona froze, afraid to move. The beast stood on hind legs, no more than six feet tall, with great green wings that matched the rest of its scaly body. But it was the monster's face that proved the most frightening feature. Eyes as black as tar peered at her from within deep reptilian sockets. The creature grinned, displaying a set of saberlike teeth, all set menacingly in slimy black gums.

Oona licked at her lips, which were suddenly very dry, and yet that was as much as she could move. It was like a bad dream, not at all what she would have expected to find on Dark Street, let alone the theater lobby.

What surprised Oona even more was when the hideous-looking beast actually spoke. The dragon reared back its head, no doubt preparing to run at her and strike. It roared, flapping its wings and beating at its chest. And then it stopped, as if the show were suddenly over. It cocked its head to one side, and then in a highly refined voice asked: "Have you a porcupine for me?"

Oona was forced to clear her throat in order to speak,

and when she did it came out in a high squeak. "Um . . . yes."

"Oh, you dear girl," the dragon said concernedly, and then used its front claws to open its large mouth, from which emerged a man's head. "Sorry about that," he said. "Didn't mean to frighten you. And you, too, dear fellow. It's only a costume, you know."

Oona swallowed, feelings of shock and amazement and anger rushing through her in quick succession. She squinted, still attempting to understand precisely what she was looking at. After a while she could see very clearly that this thing was no real dragon at all—which Oona knew from her history lessons no longer existed outside the Land of Faerie—but it was, in fact, a highly elaborate costume. A very good one, she had to admit, which only served to fuel her anger.

"Didn't mean to frighten us?" she said sharply. "If that were the truth, then why dress up in a dragon costume?"

The man lowered his head, sweeping his arm out in front of him as if taking a bow.

"All part of the show!" he exclaimed, and then disappeared behind one of the marble columns. Several seconds later he appeared on the other side of the column dressed in Roman armor with a laurel wreath crown on his head: the spitting image of Julius Caesar. The dragon costume was nowhere to be seen.

Roderick moved out from behind Oona, and the two of them shared a surprised look.

"Et tu, Brute?" asked Julius Caesar.

"I beg your pardon?" Oona asked.

Instead of answering, the man once again disappeared behind the column, only to reappear on the other side dressed in a long red dress and comely black wig. The transformation was startling, from Roman war general to medieval countess in the blink of an eye. The woman peered at Oona, her eyes encircled with thick black eye makeup, and spoke in a perfect feminine timbre. "Is this the porcupine I see before me?"

Deacon circled down from the ceiling to Oona's shoulder.

"Why, it's Lady Macbeth," he said. "Very convincing."

"This chap's mad as a hatter," said Roderick.

Lady Macbeth slipped quickly behind the column, only to emerge from the other side as none other than Oswald the Great. With long black hair and wand in hand, he pointed at the box containing the porcupine.

"Bring the animals to me, please," he said.

Oona, who was shaking her head at the sudden appearance and disappearance of all these characters, could think of nothing to do but comply with Oswald's orders.

Pancake's orders, she reminded herself. *This is not Oswald. It's Albert Pancake, the Master of Ten Thousand Faces.*

She set the box at his feet and opened it. Roderick did the same. Inside, glaring up at them, were the two porcupines, looking highly anxious. Oona only hoped that she would not be required to give hers a massage.

Oswald deftly plucked one sharp barb from each of the porcupines, and then handed one to Oona and the other to Roderick. The man nodded at her before snapping his fingers and leaping behind the column. He was gone no more than three seconds this time when he reappeared, draped in a deep blue robe, taking on the full likeness of her uncle, the Wizard. "And good luck," he said, the voice surprisingly similar to that of her uncle.

Oona gasped. It was nothing short of astounding. Down to the wrinkled nose, the man had embodied the Wizard to near perfection. Though "*near*" was the optimal word. It was the eyes that gave him away. Oona would know her uncle's eyes anywhere: wise, caring, penetrating, even mischievous—like a little boy's eyes that had seen many things. And those were not the eyes that looked at her now. That was something that could not be imitated.

"Take the porcupine barb to the tower," said the Master of Ten Thousand Faces in a remarkable imitation of the Wizard. "It is your ticket to the second part of today's challenge."

A *click* sounded behind Oona as Adler Iree came rushing through the front entrance, a box tucked under his arm. He glanced ruefully at her, giving her a grin as he paused to catch his breath, and Oona could feel her cheeks grow very warm.

When she turned back to Mr. Pancake to thank him, she saw that he no longer resembled her uncle, but now appeared to be a tutu-wearing ballerina with long golden braids, doing pirouettes.

"Get me out of this loony bin," Roderick said, and made a dash for the door.

Oona followed suit, taking only the briefest of moments to stop at Adler's side and touch his shoulder.

"Good luck," she said, and just had time to see the boy's tattooed face flush red before she rushed through the doors and back out into the daylight, feeling ecstatically alive. It had been quite bold of her to touch his shoulder in such a familiar way, and she suddenly wondered what had come over her. Whatever it was, she certainly did not have time to consider it for long.

"Samuligan!" she shouted, launching herself through the open carriage door and slamming it shut. "To the park! Isadora and Roderick have the lead. There's no time to waste!"

She fell back into her seat as the carriage surged forward, the sting of Headmistress Duvet's handiwork still throbbing down her backside as they sped along the busy street in the direction of Oswald Park.

CHAPTER TEN

Going Up

I f you know what's good for you, Roderick," Sir Baltimore shouted, "you'll win this challenge!"

Roderick's father stood below the front of the stage, a cigar clamped between his teeth, smoke pluming around his head as if he were on fire from the inside. Oona had never seen the man looking so angry, and it was all she could do to keep from looking at him as she followed close on Roderick's heels up the stage steps to the tower. Deacon landed in a nearby tree to await her return.

"That girlfriend of yours is making a fool out of you!" Sir Baltimore shouted at his son. "She's already up there! Get your hind quarters moving, or you'll disgrace the family!"

"Daddy!" little Penelope Rutherford cried at her father. "You said you would read me a story!"

The little girl held up her book and swatted her father with it in much the same manner as Headmistress Duvet had swatted Oona with the IMPROPER cane.

"Penelope!" Sir Baltimore shouted, snatching the book from her and slapping it down on the front of the stage. "I will not read any more of this faerie-tale drivel ever again if you do not shush, girl." He returned his attention to Roderick, balling one fist and shaking it in the air. "Remember what we talked about last night, son. Now go win this thing."

Oona and Roderick stopped center stage, where the architect calmly folded his newspaper and then stood. He adjusted the ridiculously tall top hat on his head as Deacon perched in one of the nearby trees.

Catching her breath, Oona glanced from Sir Baltimore to Roderick—specifically from Sir Baltimore's shaking fist to the purplish bruise on Roderick's cheek—and Oona wondered just how much "talking" had actually taken place between them last night. Sir Baltimore's fist slammed down on Penelope's book of faerie tales.

"Go get 'em, son!" he shouted. "The family is counting on you!"

Roderick did not so much as glance in his father's direction. He and Oona handed their porcupine barbs to the architect, who in turn handed them each a key.

"Take the side stairs to the fourth floor," the architect

said, indicating the outside stairs that Oona and the others had used to descend from the third floor the day before.

"That is all," the architect said, and promptly sat back down, returning his attention to his paper.

"Go! Go! Go!" Sir Baltimore cried.

Oona and Roderick took to the stairs as Adler Iree came running up the stage steps behind them. It was going to be a close race, Oona realized, taking the steps two at a time. And then she remembered that Isadora was already up there, far ahead of them all, and she began taking the steps three at a time.

Roderick was the first to reach the fourth floor, where the steps ended at a door. Oona could feel the sway of the building in the breeze, and hear the creak of nails in wood. Roderick drove his key into the door, shoving his way inside and slamming the door shut behind him.

"You rotter!" Oona called after him. She shoved her own key into the hole, shouldering the door open. As she turned to close it, she saw Adler pounding his way up the final few steps. Feeling quite a bit more chivalrous than Roderick Rutherford, she held the door open for Adler. He slipped quickly into the building, holding his frayed top hat to his head.

"What the?" Adler exclaimed. He skidded to a halt. The door clicked shut and Oona spun around.

"Oh, dear me," she said, taking it all in. "What have I gotten myself into?"

"I'm asking myself the same question," said Adler.

Adler and Oona stared. Three feet in front of them, taking up nearly the entire floor, was an open pit of snakes. The serpents writhed and wriggled, their scaly black bodies slithering over one another like a dark carpet. Oona backed against the door.

"Where is Roderick?" she asked, seeing no sign of the other boy. "And Isadora, for that matter?" she added.

"I haven't the slightest—" Adler began, but his words were cut short when something swooped past his head. He jumped back against the wall, just managing to avoid being hit by the thing's tail. "What was that?" he asked, out of breath.

Whatever it had been, it had disappeared from sight just as quickly as it had appeared. Oona craned her head back, looking toward the ceiling, only to realize that there *was* no ceiling. At least, not directly overhead. Only if she squinted could she make out some vague semblance of where the top of the room might end, some ten or more stories above.

"Look," Oona said, pointing up.

Adler peered upward, bracing himself against the wall. "Is that what they call a riverboat?" he asked.

Oona nodded. It was a riverboat indeed: a Mississippi paddle steamer, if Oona's memory served correctly. Her mother, who had been a great lover of boats of all kinds, had owned a book with illustrations, and this had been one of Oona's and her mother's favorites.

Suspended by cables from the ceiling, the magnificent white boat hung two stories above their heads, complete with round paddle wheel at the back and river barnacles clinging to the hull. How the architect had managed to fit it inside the tower eluded her at first, until she realized that this must be the spot where the tower bulged out like a snake swallowing an egg.

Speaking of snakes, Oona thought. *There's something not quite right about these serpents.*

No sooner had the thought occurred to her than one of the snakes leapt straight into the air. As if this behavior weren't startling enough, the snake suddenly unfurled a set of large black wings and then flew directly at her. She screamed, throwing her hands to her face, but the snake banked in the air, slapping the side of her head with its tail before soaring upward and disappearing over the top of the boat.

"Did you see that?" Adler asked, as if Oona might have missed it.

Before she could respond, however, she saw something else that took her by surprise. It was Roderick Rutherford peering over the edge of the boat above.

"Now, how did you get up there?" Oona asked.

Another snake leapt out of the pit and into the air, this one extending its wings and darting at Adler. Adler held up his hands, protecting his face. The snake opened its mouth in a wide yawn, displaying a horrifying set of shiny fangs. Its mouth clamped down, its fangs sinking into the brim of Adler's top hat and wrenching it from his head.

"No, you don't!" Adler shouted.

He grabbed the snake around the middle with both hands, but the snake did not slow in the least. Its tail wrapped tightly around Adler's wrists and soared upward, flapping its bizarre wings like mad, taking Adler and his top hat with it. Shouting in surprise, Adler looked down as he and the snake soared around the side of the riverboat and disappeared over the top.

"So that's how it's done, is it?" Oona said. "Seems . . . easy enough."

Sounding less than confident even to her own ears, she braced herself against the wall, attempting to steady her nerves. Seconds later she received her chance to test her theory. Another snake jumped into the air, unfurled its wings, and came straight at her . . . except there was something different about this particular snake. While all the rest of the serpents were black, this one appeared bone white—an Albino snake—with huge, pink batlike wings. Half a heartbeat later all the remaining snakes in the pit leapt into the air, unfurling hundreds of sets of black wings and chasing after the white one.

It all happened so fast that Oona didn't have time to second-guess her decision, and when the white snake swooped by within inches of her head, she reached out and grabbed hold of it. The slithering white tail wrapped itself snuggly around her wrists, and both Oona and the snake vaulted upward into the open air of the room. Only unlike Adler's snake, the white one did not head directly for the top of the boat, but instead rose halfway to the boat's hull before diving back to the ground.

Oona screamed, her insides feeling as if they had been left hovering above her. More terrifying than the wild flight, however, was the swarm of flying snakes following close behind like a mini-hurricane. Oona could see their open mouths and glistening fangs only inches from her feet.

Yet again the white snake changed directions in mid-air, shooting for the ceiling, and Oona's shoes slapped briefly against the floor as they turned. Several of the pursuing snakes crashed into the pit, but most of them managed to pull out of the dive just in time.

The white snake vaulted straight up, the swarm of black serpents like a slithering shadow at Oona's heels. The speed was incredible, her skirts nearly flattening around her legs as they flew over the boat like a bullet, past the upper deck, and then jackknifed in the air.

Oona's stomach leapt into her throat, and her arms felt like rubber. For a mere second, she thought she caught a glimpse of Isadora Iree floating in the air, and then Isadora was gone from view in the blink of an eye. Oona shook her head, assuming that she had only imagined it.

They were spiraling back down, down the side of the building, Oona's toes scraping the wall. A quick glance at her feet revealed several snakes with their mouths clamped onto the heels of her shoes.

"Oh, dear," she squeaked. "Most unsatisfactory."

She kicked at them wildly, meanwhile using her strength to pull her knees to her stomach, getting her feet as far ahead of the pursuing dark cloud as possible. But the snakes continued to close in from above, and it suddenly occurred to Oona that she was going to be sick.

Mercifully, the white snake leveled off, skimming over the top deck of the boat, nearly crashing into Adler Iree, who stood wide-eyed near one of the side rails.

"Let go!" he shouted, and then ducked as Oona and the swarm of snakes whizzed inches above his head.

"Let go?" Oona shouted back. "Are you crazy?"

The white snake turned hard left, only just avoiding a collision with the sidewall. The front half of the pursuing swarm struck the wall hard, bouncing off and wobbling in the air before drunkenly descending back to the floor. But the second half of the swarm pulled up just in time and appeared to be gaining speed. And so was the white snake.

Oona's arms began to ache as they circled the boat, around and around, gaining momentum with each revolution. The room began to lose focus. All her blood seemed to rush to her feet. Just when Oona was sure she was going to pass out, the white snake once again dove toward the top deck of the boat.

She knew what she had to do. In spite of all of her instincts to hold on, Oona released her grip, feeling completely out of control, hoping beyond hope that Adler's advice had been wiser than it sounded.

The instant she let go, the snake uncoiled from her wrists and she dropped, tumbling through the air, falling, falling . . . and landing quite perfectly into Adler Iree's outstretched arms.

"I've got you!" Adler cried, then: "Umph!"

Adler stumbled back, the two of them toppling to the deck, Oona coming to a halt in a heap of skirts on top of Adler—except, for the moment, it did not seem to Oona as if she had come to a halt at all. Everything was spinning.

She tried to focus, peering at what she thought was a face . . . with writing on it. But that was silly, why would a face have . . .

Her vision cleared, and she saw where she was: on the top deck of the riverboat, lying on top of Adler Iree, their faces less than an inch apart. She felt his breath tickle her cheek, and for an instant Oona wondered whose face might be more red, Adler's or her own.

"Thank you," Oona said, her breath shaken.

Adler brushed a stray hair from her face, and though she wouldn't have thought it possible, Oona felt her pulse quicken.

"You all right there?" Adler asked.

Oona nodded, for the moment lost in Adler's blurry-looking face—the tattoos so close. She wondered briefly at their meaning, and then suddenly good manners and decency struck home. She glanced down, saw her skirt splayed around her like a disheveled bed, and pushed herself quickly to her feet, doing her best to hold her balance. She peered over the edge of the boat. The snakes, it seemed, had ceased their maddened aerial chase and had returned to the pit several stories below.

"That was fascinating, so it was," said Adler, though whether he'd meant the ride on the winged snakes, or his and Oona's close encounter, Oona wasn't sure. She did not know what to say.

As if to break the awkward silence, Adler asked: "Where do you suppose the architect got those flying snakes from? I've never seen their like."

Oona ran a nervous hand through her hair. It was a good question, but what concerned her more was where the others had gotten to.

"Where are Roderick and Isadora?" she asked.

Adler slowly looked upward.

Following his gaze, Oona tilted her head back and received a bit of a shock. Suddenly, she remembered seeing Isadora seemingly floating in the air. It hadn't made sense at the time, but now she understood perfectly. She shook her head, wondering what they had gotten themselves into.

Twenty feet above, she could see Roderick Rutherford, and not far above Roderick was Isadora, each of them attempting to keep their footing on what appeared to be their own slowly rising carpet. Neither of them looked very confident as the floating carpets inched their way toward the high ceiling above. Roderick wobbled unsteadily, and Isadora looked as if she might topple forward at any moment, each of them attempting to hold their balance with the aid of a pine-branch broomstick.

"Flying carpets," Oona said, feeling both a surge of excitement and dread at the same moment. Here was something that she knew about from her history of magic lessons with Deacon. They were quite rare objects, Oona knew—faerie-made relics left over from before the Great Faerie War—and could also be quite dangerous if handled improperly.

"Where do we get ours?" Oona asked excitedly.

"Let's find out," Adler said, and the two of them headed to the lower deck in search of their own carpet.

They found them near the rear of the ship on the bottom deck.

Floating along the side of the riverboat were two carpets, on top of which lay one broomstick each. Oona took in a sharp breath at the sight of the beautiful enchanted objects.

She had never before seen one up close. They were exquisite in craftsmanship, which didn't come as any surprise. Anything made by faerie hands would be of only the finest quality. The pattern appeared to be woven from . . . not thread—at least not any sort of thread that Oona had ever seen—but from strands of light. Red and gold and black and blue, the strands formed marvelous patterns that reminded Oona of pixielike faces. She guessed that the carpets had been borrowed from the Museum of Magical History.

Hopefully, she thought, *these things still work properly after hundreds of years of storage.*

Remembering her promise to not use magic during the challenge, Oona reasoned that since it was not her own magic, then the rule did not apply, and since everyone else was supposed to use the carpets, then they were all still on a level playing field.

"I guess I'll take this one," Oona said, reaching over the rail and picking up the broomstick.

Adler nodded. "Ah . . . yeah. Okay," he said, before climbing over the rail and gingerly placing his foot down upon the last remaining carpet. The instant his foot touched, the carpet began slowly to rise, and Adler's eyes rounded. He quickly picked up the broomstick and, like Roderick and Isadora, held it out in front of him to keep his balance. Slowly, he began to rise up the side of the boat toward the top deck.

Oona climbed onto her own carpet, testing her footing, and feeling quite unbalanced. Her first instinct, like the others, was to use the broomstick as a balancing pole, like a high-wire performer in the circus, as the carpet began its slow assent toward the roof. But because of her magical knowledge, Oona resisted the urge, and instead spread her feet farther apart, bending her knees to steady herself against the wobble of the carpet.

"Magic carpets require stimulation," she whispered to herself.

Faeries, she remembered, had used carpets instead of horses in their war maneuvers during their battles against the Magicians of Old and the fighting men who followed them. In a book titled *The War*, Oona had seen an illustration of a thousand faerie soldiers soaring down a hillside, each of them mounted on their own magic carpet, each holding in their hands a single pine-branch broomstick.

"Why are they all holding brooms?" Oona had inquired of Samuligan one day, nearly three years ago. She had taken the book to the faerie servant, knowing that, of all beings, Samuligan would know the answer to her question, for Samuligan had once been a powerful general in the Queen of Faerie's army.

Samuligan had smiled his mischievous grin and replied: "We used them to sweep our carpets. The carpets require stimulation, you see, and the faster and steadier you sweep an enchanted carpet, the faster and steadier it will travel."

Presently, standing on her very own flying carpet, Oona grinned as she glanced upward to see that none of the other contestants possessed the knowledge that she did. And so Oona began to sweep, slowly at first, as her balance was quite unsteady, but the more times she swept the surface of the carpet, the higher and faster she began to climb, and so, too, did her balance improve. Indeed, the more momentum she gained, the easier it was to keep her equilibrium.

In no time at all she had passed up Adler, who was presently facing the opposite direction, fighting for balance, and did not see Oona rise up past him.

This is going quite well, she thought, and found that it was not only a nice boost to her hopes of gaining a lead over the others, but that it was also quite fun.

From just above her, however, she heard Roderick shout: "I see what you're doing!"

Oona looked up to find Roderick peering down at her, fighting for balance as he turned his head up and shouted: "Isadora, my lady! Use the broom to sweep the carpet! That's the missing clue!"

"The missing clue?" Oona said, wondering what Roderick had meant.

When Roderick made no reply, she realized there was no time to ponder and began to sweep more rapidly in an attempt to pass Roderick before he could get his carpet moving any faster. But in her sudden panic to gain speed, her sweeping became more erratic than smooth and steady, causing her to lose her balance.

She flailed her arms as the carpet listed to the left like a raft struck by a wave. In her attempt to catch her balance, she nearly dropped the broomstick. She felt it slide from her grip before she was able to catch it again at the very tip of the handle. In the meantime she had lost some of her momentum, allowing both Isadora and Roderick to multiply their speed above her.

Thanking her good fortune that she had managed to keep hold of the broom, Oona once again began to sweep the carpet, this time steadily increasing her pace. It was working. Her carpet was gaining on Roderick's, only now that Roderick had figured out the secret of sweeping his carpet with his broom, he was rising nearly as fast as Oona.

And now Oona could hear a third broom sweeping, and she knew precisely where it was coming from. She could see Isadora above them all, rising steadily toward the ceiling.

Oona began to sweep faster, careful not to break her rhythm. She was advancing on Roderick, her hands slipping into a powerful rhythm, which reminded her of her assent to the top of the Goblin Tower three months past, beating on a hand drum during her assent to the top of the tower: one, two, three, four, one, two, three, four. And now, here she was once again, traveling through the inside of a tower, only this time she was not in the company of four lazy goblins but in a race against the likes of Roderick Rutherford, whom she was presently neck and neck with, and Isadora Iree, whom they were both gaining on.

Oona's glowing carpet had begun to pulse like a beating heart, nearly surpassing Roderick's, when a fourth broom joined the rhythmic swish of the others. Adler had figured out the sweeping secret and was now working steadily away, but unless one of them made an unrecoverable mistake, Oona knew that he was too far behind to catch up.

It was now a three-way race between Oona, Roderick, and Isadora, whose lead was about to be overtaken. Oona's and Roderick's carpets rose side by side as they came up even with Isadora, the fine young lady's normally perfectly composed face now flushed red with the exertion of sweeping. Oona wondered earnestly if Isadora had ever partaken in such a domestic activity in her life, but the thought passed as quickly as a sweep of a broom.

She could see the finish line coming up fast. A round wooden walkway encircled the outer wall about thirty feet above them. Frustration gripped at Oona's insides as she realized that the exit was positioned on the side of the walkway closest to where Isadora was headed. But Oona planned to get there first.

She started to sweep so energetically that the static electricity caused her skirt to stick to the bristles of the broom each time it swooped past. This was it. She was gaining. She was going to pass them both.

And then it happened. A wobble. A jerk. And Oona

felt as if she were about to fall. Her carpet jolted to one side, threatening to throw her off, and it was all she could do to keep her balance. Her heart leapt into her throat as a cry of panic shot from between her lips. Luckily, her upward momentum was so strong that the carpet did not throw her off completely.

She took in a great gasp of air, steadying herself, and just as she began to wonder what had happened, she felt a second jolt even worse than the first. This time Oona was more on her guard, and not only did she manage to keep herself from being bucked off by the sudden violent movement, but she was able to see the cause of the carpet's malfunction—which turned out not to be a malfunction after all.

Roderick had temporarily stopped sweeping, and was instead using his broomstick to whack at Oona's carpet in an attempt to knock it out from beneath her feet.

Oona gasped. "You bloody bully! You, sir, are no gentleman!"

Roderick paid her no mind. Clearly satisfied that his attempt to knock Oona from the air had at least managed to impede her progress, he once again began to sweep his own carpet.

For a moment Oona had a good mind to take a swing at Roderick with her own broomstick, but, thinking better of the situation, she realized that that might be exactly what Roderick hoped she would do: waste more time trying to get even, while he and Isadora gained even more of a lead than they already had.

Oona squared her shoulders, squeezed down hard on the broom handle, and once again began to sweep—long steady strokes that grew faster and more precise. She quickly realized that this was not a game of strength so much as it was one of timing, rhythm, and stamina.

Her arms and shoulders were beginning to ache, her muscles pulling tight beneath her skin like steel cables. She pushed resiliently through the discomfort, biting back the pain, and began once again to gain on her opponents. The space between them narrowed more and more, and for several seconds Oona could taste a juicy slice of hope. It was still possible that she might win.

But the taste of hope abruptly evaporated, only to be replaced by the bitterness of frustration and doubt.

Despite Oona's fevered effort, it was Isadora who reached the top first, her carpet coasting to a smooth and seemingly practiced stop along the edge of the rickety wooden walkway. Oona felt like screaming in irritation as Isadora stepped nimbly from her carpet and hurried toward the exit.

Roderick was the next to arrive at the top, but when his carpet came to a shuttering halt, he stepped leisurely to the extended walkway, not appearing to be in any great hurry whatsoever to overtake Isadora—a behavior that Oona found most peculiar, considering how fervent Roderick's father had been that he should come in first.

Oona was in an altogether different state of mind. In that moment, she wanted more than anything to beat Isadora to the door, no matter how unrealistic it might have seemed. She could see the distance between them was too great. Isadora had too much of a lead for Oona to make up the distance, yet she leapt to the walkway mere seconds after Roderick and ran full out, shoes clonking against the planks of wood.

Isadora tried the door, but it would not open. She began fumbling with the key that the architect had given them at the beginning of the challenge, attempting to jam it into the lock before the others could catch up.

Oona's heart skipped a beat. For an instant she thought maybe, just maybe, she might have a chance. Yes. It was there: the slimmest possibility that she could get to the door just as Isadora pulled it open, and Oona could slip through the opening before the other girl had time even to know what was happening. She could almost taste the victory, but unfortunately, Roderick was between them. He placed himself purposefully right in front of Oona, blocking her path to the door . . . and that was all it took.

In the few seconds that Roderick held Oona up—sticking his arms straight out like a cross, and moving first to one side of the walkway and then to the other—Isadora yanked her key from the lock, flinging the door wide open. A stream of sunlight spilled across her smug face as she held the key over her head like a victory trophy and, to Oona's dismay, once again immerged first from the tower doorway, the winner of another day's challenge.

To Oona, it all seemed like a bad dream. Roderick Rutherford, as had happened the day before, emerged only seconds after Isadora, finishing in second place, leaving Oona to step through the doorway in third.

As she exited the tower, squinting against the bright sunlight, Oona was forced to suppress a shout of indignation. Isadora grinned triumphantly in Oona's direction as the architect handed the fine young lady yet another blue ribbon, and Oona could do nothing but weakly smile back. She had lost again, and it was simply insufferable.

CHAPTER ELEVEN

Oona and Adler

I'm thinkin' my sister's cheating," said Adler. "And now I'm out of the contest."

The two of them, Adler and Oona, sat side by side on the curb, watching the spectators exit the gates outside Oswald Park. Deacon had taken his customary place on Oona's shoulder. In the distance, the Magician's Tower pointed to the sky like a disjointed finger.

Oona could only hope that Headmistress Duvet from the Academy of Fine Young Ladies did not happen by, as it was highly unladylike to sit on the sidewalk with one's feet resting on an iron utility-hole cover in the street. But at the moment, Oona didn't care. In her hand she held the second white ribbon she'd received from the architect, which contained the clue for the next day's challenge. She had scarcely looked at it.

"I'm sorry, what did you say?" Oona asked. It was hard for her to concentrate on anything at the moment, even Adler Iree's charming Irish-accented voice.

"I said, I think Isadora is cheating," he replied. "But I can't figure out how."

They sat in silence for a long moment, watching the spectators disperse. Among the crowd were Sir Baltimore Rutherford, his daughter Penelope, and Roderick. Sir Baltimore looked more furious than ever. His normally impeccable hair was standing up at the edges as if he had been pulling at it with his fists.

"Will you read to me now, Daddy?" Penelope asked as they exited through the park gates.

To Oona's surprise, Sir Baltimore snatched the book from his daughter's small hands and tossed it violently into the air. The book sailed nearly twenty yards over the fence and plunked down in a stand of thorny bushes.

"Daddy!" Penelope began to cry. "My book! How are you going to read to me now?"

The spectators began to stop and stare, pointing at the family squabble and murmuring in low voices.

"I don't need that bloody book!" Sir Baltimore shouted at his daughter. "I've read it to you a hundred times. I can remember every annoying word!"

"Don't take out your anger on Penelope, Father," Roderick said. "I'm the one you're angry at."

"You're bloody well right, I'm angry at you!" Sir Baltimore howled. "That's twice you've lost. And for no good reason! What are you trying to do, ruin our family? Just wait till we get home. Why I should . . . should . . ." But when he realized he had an audience, Sir Baltimore trailed off. He picked Penelope up in one strong arm and trudged past the onlookers, leaving Roderick behind.

"What about my book?" Penelope cried.

"Hush about your bloody book. I'll buy you another one," Sir Baltimore said, then glancing back at Roderick, he added: "If I can even afford it."

This last bit he said mostly to himself, but his carriage was parked very near where Oona and Adler sat at the curb.

Just then, Isadora Iree glided through the park entrance accompanied by her mother, as well as Headmistress Duvet and several younger members of the academy. None of them so much as glanced in Oona's direction, and Oona was thankful. She didn't feel much like sharing polite smiles with people who disapproved of her.

She, Adler, and Deacon watched as Roderick approached Isadora, took her hand, and bowed. Isadora curtsied.

"Well played, my lady," Roderick said.

"You, too," Isadora replied, and when she removed her hand from Roderick's, Oona caught a glimpse of something in Isadora's hand.

"A note," Oona said.

"What?" asked Adler.

"A note," Oona repeated. "Roderick just passed Isadora a note."

Adler rolled his eyes. "Oh. Probably another of his love poems."

"You know about the poems?" Oona asked timidly, wondering how Adler felt about such things.

"Oh, aye," Adler said. "I haven't read them, so I can't say if they're any good. Isadora says they are for *girlfriend eyes* only. Whatever that means."

Oona blushed. She thought she knew exactly what Isadora meant by girlfriend eyes only, and she had a moment's fantasy of one day receiving her own letter from Adler meant for Oona's "girlfriend eyes" only.

"Roderick, let's go!" Sir Baltimore shouted.

Roderick gave Isadora a shrug, and then the two of them parted, Roderick heading to his father's carriage and Isadora and her entourage moving in the opposite direction up the street.

Oona watched the ladies until they had disappeared in the crowd, resisting the urge to follow. One of them, either Madame Iree or Isadora herself, was likely in possession of the Punchbowl Oracle. Oona would have loved nothing more than to catch them at their cheating as they pulled the bowl from its secret hiding place.

"There is a rumor going around," said Adler, "that Sir Baltimore has quite a bit of money at stake on this contest."

Oona raised an eyebrow. "You think he's bet for Roderick to win?"

Adler tipped his top hat back. "It would explain that attitude of his, so it would: why he's so upset at Roderick coming in second and all."

Oona thought of the bruise on Roderick's cheek. "Do you think Sir Baltimore would actually strike his own son over the loss of a little money?"

"Who says it's a *little* money?" Adler asked.

Deacon cleared his throat. "It would not be the first time Sir Baltimore were to get himself into trouble over a bet. I believe he has lost quite a bit of money to a certain criminal organization over the years."

"You mean Red Martin and his Nightshade Corporation?" Oona asked.

"The very same," said Deacon. "It is said that the Rutherfords were once much wealthier than they are now. And Red Martin's pockets are much fatter for it."

"It's mostly because of Sir Baltimore's so-called *eidetic memory*, so it is," said Adler. "It's not so perfect after all."

"Very true," replied Deacon.

"His what?" Oona asked, unfamiliar with the term.

"Eidetic memory," Deacon said. "It means a perfect memory. Sometimes referred to as 'total recall.' And more recently, since the invention of the camera, it has been known as a 'photographic memory.'"

"Oh, yes," Oona said. "I remember his boasting about his memory at the party the other evening. How he had inherited it."

Adler shook his head. "Yeah, to be sure. It's his claim to fame. Except Sir Baltimore doesn't seem to have such a good memory as his father and grandfather had."

"But what does that have to do with gambling?" Oona asked.

"He uses his extraordinary memory to his advantage when playing cards," said Deacon. "But playing cards is not a science."

Oona shook her head at the irresponsibility of such frivolous gambling, but knew that Sir Baltimore would not have been the first man or woman to lose large sums of money to Red Martin. Even now, with Red Martin in hiding, his Nightshade Hotel and Casino still operated freely, continuing to dig deep into the pockets of the street's unwise gamblers.

The thought reminded Oona again of how the Punch-bowl Oracle was just the sort of thing that a scoundrel like Red Martin would love to get his hands on. But surely it wasn't he who was behind the theft. How could it be, when so far all of the evidence—the fact that Isadora kept winning the challenges, and that Madame Iree's ring had been found beneath the caravan—pointed to the dressmaker and her daughter? She wondered if perhaps Adler might know something, or at least might know a place where the ladies might keep such an object.

"How do you suppose Isadora's doing it?" Oona asked. "How is she getting the answers?"

"Haven't the foggiest," said Adler. "But she's not getting those clues on her own. I just don't believe it."

"Well, there are no rules saying you can't have help," Oona pointed out.

"Help is one thing," Adler said. "But she's got the *answers*. Somehow, she knows them ahead of time."

Oona considered whether or not to let Adler in on the disappearance of the Punchbowl Oracle. She thought the matter through very carefully before finally deciding to tell him everything she knew, including her suspicions that Adler's own mother was the thief. After all, Adler was now out of the competition, leaving only herself, Roderick, and Isadora to compete the following day. She turned to Adler, met his handsome gaze, and the story spilled out of her.

When she had finished, Adler began to shake his head. "I just don't see it happening."

"Which part?' Oona asked.

"Well," Adler said, "the part about my mother crawling beneath the gypsy caravan wearing one of her prized dresses."

Oona nodded. "Well, it is only a theory. But how do you explain her ring being found under the wagon?"

"That I don't know," Adler said. His brow furrowed as he thought, and Oona found the expression exceptionally cute. At last he said: "I know what you're thinking."

Oona's heart gave a sudden thump in her chest, and her face went bright red. But when Adler continued, she realized that he had not actually been reading her mind, and had not been referring to her thoughts about his cuteness.

"You're wondering, if my mother did steal that bleeding punchbowl," he said, "then why would she give the answers to Isadora and not to me?"

"The thought had occurred to me," Oona admitted, feeling somewhat guilty, even though she hadn't been the one who had brought it up, and for an instant she was tempted to place her hand on top of Adler's to comfort him. Remembering that they were out in public, however, she restrained herself.

Adler nodded gravely. "Well, I actually don't think

she would. But then again, I do know that those who attend the Academy of Fine Young Ladies swear some sort of oath of loyalty to the other members. That being the case . . ." He trailed off.

It was Deacon who finished his thought for him. "That being the case, then it would be out of a sense of duty that she would give the answers to her daughter and not to her son."

Adler nodded solemnly. "That, and the fact that I wouldn't want to win by cheating, anyway. She would know that."

Oona suddenly beamed at Adler, completely forgetting all sense of decorum and placing her hand on top of his, despite the very open display of affection she was showing out in public toward a boy she hardly knew, and giving it a squeeze. "I didn't think you would," she said.

For several long seconds, their eyes met, locking in place, and Oona's fingers tingled. It seemed to Oona that, if she weren't careful, she might actually fall into those blue eyes of his and be lost forever.

Deacon made an uncomfortable throat-clearing sound, and Oona shook her head as if coming out of a hypnotic trance. She quickly removed her hand from Adler's. Adler cleared his own throat, and Oona could still feel the tingle in her hand.

"I still don't think my mother would have stolen that

punchbowl, Miss Crate," he said. "I don't know how that ring of hers got where it did, but to think of her crawling beneath that caravan and through some trapdoor? Just doesn't sound like something she's capable of."

Oona nodded. It was indeed an almost comical thought: imagining Madame Iree crawling in the dirt and forcing her voluptuous form through that trapdoor. Indeed, now that Oona considered it, she wasn't sure if Madame Iree *could* have squeezed through, even if she hadn't been wearing the voluminous dress. Her prodigious bosom alone might have even eliminated her as a suspect.

"I'll have a look around the house, though," Adler said. "If Isadora is using the punchbowl to cheat— whether with the help of my mother or not—our house would be as likely a place to hide it as any. She lives at home on the weekends."

"That would be excellent," Oona said. "Meanwhile, I'll have another look around the caravan. See if I can't get any more information from Madame Romania from Romania."

Deacon adjusted his position on her shoulder. "Or, alternatively, you could spend the rest of the day with that contest clue."

He poked his beak in the direction of Oona's hands. Oona held up the white ribbon imprinted with the following day's clue. Pulling the ribbon taut, she read the clue out loud.

"Closely consider the reverse, and be careful not to get mixed up."

Flipping the clue over, Oona revealed a set of letters on the reverse side of the ribbon that made no sense to her whatsoever.

TL GL GSV XOLXPNZPVI

"Another anagram, perhaps," Oona said.

"Just what I was thinking," said Deacon.

Oona considered the letters a moment before nodding. "You're absolutely right, Deacon. This is going to require some serious concentration." She stood up from the curb and placed the clue into her pocket, before adding: "Just as soon as we confer with Madame Romania from Romania."

Deacon sighed.

CHAPTER TWELVE

The Tick-Tock Society

U pon departing company from Adler Iree, Oona felt a twinge of sadness: a faint, almost invisible melancholy accompanied by a jittery feeling in her chest. She'd never felt anything like it before and, likewise, couldn't believe how bold she had been to place her hand on top of Adler's. Especially out in public.

Having attended the Midnight Masquerade with him three months ago was one thing, where holding hands with a dance partner was perfectly acceptable behavior. But her actions this afternoon had been quite uncontrolled, and she wondered what Adler must have been thinking.

He didn't pull his hand away, she thought. *But then*

again, it's not usually the girl who is supposed to make such moves toward the boy, but the other way around.

And now that she thought of it, perhaps Adler had been offended. Maybe he hadn't moved his hand only because he hadn't wanted to embarrass her. What if he had run off and was looking for a place to wash his hand at that very moment?

What a ridiculous idea, she thought to herself, and then: *But what if it's true?*

Consumed by her whirlwind of thoughts, Oona walked absently through the park, momentarily oblivious to where she was. Not so long ago, Oona would have scarcely set foot upon the park grounds for fear of conjuring up dreadful memories. But all at once it hit her where she was, and she nearly froze.

Instead, her steps hastened, speeding her past the spot where, three years before, she had crash-landed after the explosion of magic sent her flying: the very place she had been when her mother and sister had died beneath the fallen tree. It felt all at once disrespectful to have crossed its path, and a feeling of guilt washed over her, erasing all thoughts of Adler Iree and handholding. Such things seemed unimportant compared to her current purpose of finding the punchbowl, and receiving the answers she so desperately desired.

Several minutes later, with that feeling of tightness

still lingering in her stomach, she circled around the front of the tower, then made her way to the back of the painted gypsy wagon, where she knocked on the caravan door. There was no answer. She knocked several more times, but Madame Romania from Romania did not seem to be within.

"I wonder where she might be," Oona said.

"I don't know," Deacon said, "but perhaps this is a sign that you need to concentrate on that contest clue. If you figure it out ahead of time, then it won't matter that Isadora is using this so-called Punchbowl Oracle."

Oona bit at her lip, unwilling to reveal to Deacon that her main interest in finding the bowl was more personal than winning a contest.

She sighed. "You're right, Deacon. We'll return to Pendulum House and figure this thing out."

Though which thing, the clue on the ribbon, or the mystery of the missing punchbowl, she did not say.

"But first," she said, "Let's have a look below."

She squatted down to get a better look at the trapdoor beneath the wagon. And now that she had a chance to study it more closely, she realized that it was not only large enough for even the likes of Madame Iree to crawl through, but that there was a simple latch mechanism beneath, which would have made it quite easy to open from the outside.

Deciding to test her theory, she shuffled beneath the wagon and reached for the latch.

"What do you think you are doing?" said a voice before Oona could push the latch to the open position.

The high, irritating voice grated on Oona's ears like the squeal of a baby pig. She recognized it even before turning around.

"Inspector White," she said, scooting out from beneath the caravan and brushing herself off. "How nice to see you."

"Don't hand me any of that poppycock!" the inspector said, his pale face a mask of indignation. "I can see with my very own eyes what you were doing!"

Oona's face flushed. "It's not what it looked like," she tried.

"You can't fool me, Miss Crate," said the inspector. "You were looking for this!"

He held out a book, as if it were evidence before the court.

"I was?" she asked, feeling quite confused, her brow furrowing.

"Yes, I found this book in the bushes back there," the inspector said, jerking his thumb over his shoulder, and Oona realized that what he had found was the book of faerie tails that Sir Baltimore had taken from his daughter and thrown over the park fence. "You do realize," the inspector continued, "that littering is a highly punishable crime on our street."

"Littering?" Oona said. "But it's not my book."

The inspector shook his ghostly finger in front of Oona before using it to tap his forehead. "I'm not that stupid, Miss Crate. Why would you be looking for the book beneath that wagon if it wasn't yours?"

"I wasn't looking for . . ." Oona began, but trailed off, not wanting to explain that what she had actually been doing was tampering with the trapdoor to the caravan. Thinking better of the situation, she changed tactics. "I mean, you're absolutely right, Inspector," she said. "I've been looking all over for my book of faerie tales."

The inspector glanced down at the book, as if ready to catch Oona in a lie. His face drew out long with disappointment.

"Yes. Faerie tales, indeed," he said, and handed the book to Oona. "Now, I just have to decide whether to make an example out of you or not."

"Example?" Oona said. "For what?"

"For littering, my dear!" he exclaimed, and began cracking his knuckles one by one. "We take cleanliness very seriously here on Dark Street, unlike outside the gates in that filthy New York."

"But I wasn't littering," Oona said quickly, and thought of the best on-the-spot lie she could come up with. "Deacon and I were simply playing a game of fetch."

"Fetch?" Deacon said indignantly.

"Fetch?" said the inspector.

"Yes, fetch," Oona said. "I was throwing the book, and Deacon was bringing it back to me."

"Why, I never—" Deacon began, but was abruptly cut short when Oona nudged him with the side of her head.

"Oh . . . well, in that case," the inspector said, eying Deacon suspiciously. "There is no law against playing fetch. In fact, I play it with my wife quite often."

"With your . . . wife?" Oona said, not sure if she was more surprised to find that the inspector was married, or that he treated his spouse like a pet. "How . . . um . . . very nice," Oona said, and then: "We'll just be leaving now."

"Oh, yes," said Deacon, taking no precaution to hide his sarcasm. "Let's go play more fetch, Miss Crate. You know how I do love it so! Simply can't get enough."

"Have fun," the inspector called after them as Oona hurriedly made her way toward the park gates, tucking young Penelope's book of faerie tales beneath one arm. "And remember," the inspector shouted, "that littering is a crime!"

"You never told me the inspector was married, Deacon," Oona said under her breath.

"I thought you knew," Deacon replied.

"To anyone I would know?" Oona asked.

187

"I don't believe you have ever been introduced," Deacon said. "Though she was at the party the other evening. Mrs. Talley White. She was the one wearing the dress similar to Madame Iree's."

Oona stopped at the park entrance. "Oh, yes. I do remember. Isadora was so upset about it. Though I can't really blame her. The dress was a near perfect copy of Madame Iree's. What they call a complete knockoff. In fact, I remember mistaking her for the real Madame Iree. That was Inspector White's wife?"

"Indeed," said Deacon.

Oona paused before hesitantly saying: "And . . . the two of them play . . . fetch?"

Deacon shuttered, and Oona shook her head, attempting to erase the ridiculous image forever from her mind.

Deacon cleared his throat. "Perhaps you can return that book to Penelope Rutherford the next time you see her."

Oona slipped the book from beneath her arm.

"That's a fine idea," she said, thinking of how pleased the girl would be to have her book back. Though Penelope grated on Oona's nerves, Oona still didn't believe that Sir Baltimore should have thrown the book so cruelly over the fence. The man had a temper, to be sure, the fuse of which appeared to be quite short.

Presently, as she and Deacon exited through the park gates, Oona's eyes scanned the book cover. Written in large, spiraling script, the title read: *The Book of Long-Lost Faerie Tales: Fifty Highly Obscure Stories for Bedtime*. Edited by Michael Nerdling.

Though Oona had never been interested in faerie tales herself, having preferred books about science and facts, she couldn't help but wonder what made these particular stories so obscure. Curious, she had no sooner opened the book's cover when Deacon suddenly shouted in her ear so loudly that she nearly dropped the book entirely.

"Look out!"

Oona came to an abrupt halt, only to discover that she had just managed to avoid a collision with the fattest man she had ever seen. The man was leaning casually on the front wheel of her carriage, presently engaged in a lively conversation with Samuligan. The faerie servant sat in the high driver's seat, his cowboy hat shading his face and looking all the part of a mystical gunslinger.

The fat man, Oona knew, was none other than Mr. Barnaby B. Berkshire Bop, the senior undersecretary for the Magicians Legal Alliance. She recalled how Mr. Bop had been in fifth place only yesterday during the first part of the tower contest before backing out of the physical challenge at the last moment. Oona suppressed a smile at the thought of Mr. Bop attempting to jump from bits of hanging furniture while evading flying fruit and manic apes.

"How do you do, Mr. Bop?" Oona asked.

Mr. Bop spun suddenly around, forcing Oona to jump back in order to keep from being bopped by Mr. Bop's bulging belly.

"Oh, dear me!" said Mr. Bop, his top hat threatening to topple from his bald head.

A large mouth framed by shaggy side-whiskers smiled generously at Oona, his abundant jowls jiggling beneath a fleshy chin. Covered in an intricate map of tattooed symbols, it was Mr. Bop's face that Oona found to be his most striking characteristic. With the left half inked in shiny gold and the right half drawn in silver, the ancient swirls and runes made it nearly impossible to see the color of skin beneath. "You did give me a fright," the enormously fat man said. His voice was low and rough, yet jovial all at the same time.

Samuligan snapped his fingers. The sound was like thunder and caused Mr. Bop to jump a second time. Luckily for Oona, he jumped back instead of forward.

"Mr. Bop was just telling me a fantastic story," Samuligan said in his hushed, sly tone, and Oona saw that, in the instant he had snapped his fingers, the faerie servant was suddenly no longer wearing his cowboy hat, but instead was sporting a powdered wig upon his head, the likes of which were worn by English judges. Oona found it most comical.

"He was explaining to me," Samuligan continued, "how he is a member of the infamous Tic-Tock Society, and how one becomes a member."

"Really?" Oona asked, her interest suddenly piqued.

The Tick-Tock Society was one of the most secret societies in the entire world—so secret that, according to rumors, most of its members knew absolutely nothing of what the society was about or did. To Oona's highly rational mind, it was a ridiculous rumor, to say the least, and yet coming across an admitted member—especially one willing to speak of its secrets—was so uncommon that Oona was suddenly all ears.

"It is a simple process to become a member," Mr. Bop said, tipping back his hat and scratching at his bald head. "One merely finds a society member and asks them if they would like a cup of tomato juice. If the society member agrees that they would indeed enjoy a cup of tomato juice, the inductee must then hand the member an envelope full of birdseed. The society member then removes the birdseed from the envelope and asks for a spoonful of black pepper. The inductee must offer a grapefruit instead. If all of this is done correctly, the society member will then ask the inductee if they have seen the morning's headlines, to which the inductee must reply that they forgot to bring the sugar, but would the member accept this rattlesnake instead? To which the society member replies that

Yorkshire ham is best in winter. If the inductee agrees that Yorkshire ham is indeed best in winter, then . . ."

Oona cleared her throat as loudly as possible, causing Mr. Bop to trail off midsentence.

"How, um, exactly long does this go on, Mr. Bop?" Oona asked, her interest in the Tick-Tock Society suddenly growing very thin.

"How long?" asked Mr. Bop. "Why, it can go on for days, sometimes weeks. Indeed, one inductee, whose name I cannot share with you, has been attempting to join for four years. It all depends on the member you offer the tomato juice to."

"And how is the inductee supposed to know all of these obscure responses to all of these ridiculous questions?" Oona asked.

Mr. Bop's eyebrows rose, as if taking offense. "First off, I would not call the initiation rites of the society ridiculous. And secondly, to answer your question, all of the correct responses can be found in the Member's Handbook."

"And how does one get a Member's Handbook?" Oona asked.

Mr. Bop laughed, as if she were simply being silly. "Why, one must be a member to get a handbook. Thus the name: Member's Handbook."

"If that is the case," Oona said, struggling to keep

her agitation from reaching her voice, "then how is anyone who is not *already* a member supposed to *become* a member?"

"I don't follow you," said Mr. Bop.

"No, I didn't think you would," Oona said.

"But you ask marvelous questions," said Mr. Bop.

Oona had to concentrate very hard to keep from rolling her eyes. "Yes, thank you," she said, and then on a whim she asked: "Mr. Bop. Did you enjoy the party the other night?"

Mr. Bop once again scratched at his head, which, instead of sporting the top hat, was now topped with the judge's wig that Samuligan had been wearing previously. Oona threw Samuligan a reproachful glance, but the faerie servant's grin only widened beneath Mr. Bop's top hat. Mr. Bop did not appear to have noticed the switch.

"The party at the park?" he asked. "Indeed I did. In fact, I had a most wonderful session with that fortune-teller lady, Madame Romania from Romania."

Oona's eyes widened with excitement. Here was another person who had had contact with the gypsy woman. "Did you go into the caravan, Mr. Bop? Did she show you the Punchbowl Oracle?"

"The punchbowl what?" Mr. Bop asked.

"Oracle," Oona said. "A crystal bowl about thirteen inches in diameter."

Mr. Bop shook his head. "I did enter the caravan, yes. Quite cramped, to say the very least, yet I saw nothing of a punchbowl. She simply read my palm and told me to beware the corned beef, which I have so far managed to avoid . . . though this morning it was a near miss."

Mr. Bop let go with a tremendous laugh, and this time his belly actually did bop Oona, bouncing her against the side of the wagon wheel.

Oona rubbed agitatedly at the back of her head and frowned. She had struck the carriage quite hard, but the joke had missed her completely. Indeed, as Mr. Bop bid them all good day, and then began to lumber his way down the street, Oona stared suspiciously after him, watching his figure split through the foot traffic like an enormous ship cutting through the sea. As she watched him go, she could not help but wonder if there had been a joke at all.

"The Tick-Tock Society," Oona mused aloud. "Simply preposterous!"

CHAPTER THIRTEEN

The Cryptogram

Propped up on her pillow, Oona stared at the letters imprinted on the back of the white ribbon.

TL GL GSV XOLXPNZPVI

The letters blurred, came back into focus, and blurred again. In the distance, a clock tower chimed twelve. At the north end of the street, the Iron Gates would be opening for one minute upon New York City.

The bedcovers lay in a heap at the foot of the bed, on top of which sat Penelope Rutherford's book of obscure faerie tales. Oona toed the book cover absently. Her eyes drooped and then fluttered open, peering fixedly at the ribbon in her hand.

"Perhaps Mr. Bop stole the punchbowl," she said sleepily. "He was inside the caravan, after all. And just because he says he didn't see it doesn't mean he is telling the truth. I shall have to ask Madame Romania from Romania if she remembers his visit."

"What you have to do," Deacon intoned from his perch on her bedpost, "is figure out that clue."

Oona sighed. "Do you remember that splotch of mud on Roderick Rutherford's jacket the night of the party?"

Deacon shook his head discouragingly. "I do, and I am fairly certain it will not help you to solve that anagram."

Oona's gaze darted to Deacon, and a very tired smile creased her lips. She waved the ribbon in the air like a flag.

"This, Deacon, is not an anagram. Of that, I am quite sure."

"How can you be so certain?" he asked.

Oona flipped the ribbon over so that the front side faced Deacon. "Can you read that?"

Deacon cleared his throat. "It says: 'Closely consider the reverse, and be careful not to get mixed up.'"

"Precisely," Oona said. "It's a clue. A clue to the clue. A clue-clue."

"How clever," Deacon said, his tone dripping with sarcasm.

"I thought so," Oona replied. "Then again, I'm very

tired. Anyway, it says not to get mixed up. Well, if I'm not supposed to mix up the clue, then it's most certainly not an anagram, which is nothing but words with their letters all mixed up."

"Ah, I see," Deacon said. "So the clue is telling you *not* to try to mix the letters up. But if it is not an anagram, then what?"

"I believe it is some sort of cipher," Oona said.

"A code?" said Deacon.

"A cryptogram, to be precise," Oona said. "Each of these letters represents some other letter, or perhaps a number, depending on the cipher—in other words, the method—used to create the code. A cryptogram is therefore harder to solve than an anagram, as it is much more complex than simply rearranging the letters in front of you."

"Unless you know what method was used to create it," Deacon observed.

"That goes without saying," Oona said. "Knowing the cipher is what it is all about. Once the code is cracked, the meaning of the seemingly random letters becomes clear."

"Have you any theories?" Deacon asked, growing excited with a fervent flap of his wings.

Oona, however, appeared to be dozing off, the day's events catching hold of her in soft, lulling hands and pushing her eyelids to half-mast. Her arms ached from the ride on the flying snake, and her mind grew bleary. She yawned, and then blinked rapidly, fighting to stay awake.

"I have many theories," she said. "But until I have more data I can't say *who* stole the punchbowl."

"The punchbowl?" said Deacon, either unwilling or unable to hide his frustration. "I was speaking of the code in your hands."

"Yes, of course you were," Oona said, her head sinking into her pillow.

Deacon cocked his head to one side, thoughtfully. "You could try using the most famous of all ciphers. The Caesar Cipher—used by Julius Caesar himself—in which each letter represents a . . ."

But Oona did not hear what the letters represented. Sleep consumed her, dropping over her like a heavy cloak, forcing her down into the deepest of dream-filled slumbers. She dreamed of Mr. Bop swimming in a giant crystal punchbowl that overflowed with tomato juice; and of Headmistress Duvet, whose hair writhed with white snakes as she chased Oona down the street with her cane; except in the dream, the word *Improper* written on the paddle had been replaced with the word *Alphabet*.

Finally, Headmistress Duvet caught up to Oona in front of the Glass Gates. As the headmistress raised the paddle, Oona reached into her pocket and extracted a hand mirror, using it to shield her face from the blow. On the back of the mirror was printed the letters:

TL GL GSV XOLXPNZPVI

Oona screamed as the paddle collided with the mirror and both objects exploded into hundreds of pieces. Behind her, the Glass Gates erupted into a raining wall of shattered crystal. From behind the wall, Lady Macbeth appeared, looking wild with lunacy. She touched Oona's shoulder before asking if she would like her palm read. When Oona explained that she must find out if she was truly innocent of her mother's death, Lady Macbeth changed into the architect, who spilled a bowl of soup on her, ruining her dress and sending her toppling into his open satchel.

Oona awoke with a start, sitting bolt upright before hastily searching her bed for the ribbon with the clue. She found it on the floor. The morning sun streamed in through the window, exposing a sea of dust particles as they drifted lazily through the light. Oona snatched the ribbon from the floor, the dust swirling about her head like a halo of stars.

Deacon stirred from his perch on the bedpost. "Good morning," he announced.

Oona did not return the greeting, but only stared

hard at the ribbon and the cryptogram imprinted there. She flipped the ribbon over, rereading the clue-clue aloud.

"Closely consider the reverse, and be careful not to get mixed up." She snapped her fingers, startling Deacon into full wakefulness.

"Of course," she said. "How could I have missed it?"

She remembered the image in her dream, that of Headmistress Duvet's paddle emblazoned with the word *Alphabet*, and then the mirror that Oona had used in her own defense: the mirror with the cryptogram printed on its backside. The word *Alphabet* had broken the code. The code on the mirror. And what did mirrors do? They showed one's reflection, of course. But they also showed things not as they truly were, but in . . .

"Reverse!" she said. "Consider the reverse. It doesn't mean the reverse side of the ribbon. Deacon, fetch me some paper and a pencil. Quickly!"

"Fetch?" Deacon said, clearly disliking the word.

"Now, Deacon!" Oona said, waving her hand in a get-a-move-on gesture.

Deacon flapped to the dressing table, where he snatched up a slip of paper and a pencil nearly worn down to the nub. A few seconds later they were in Oona's lap. She grabbed the book of faerie tales at the foot of her bed for something hard to write on and quickly wrote out the entire alphabet on the paper. Below this she immediately began writing out the same letters, only in reverse.

```
A B C D E F G H I J K L M N O P Q R S T U V W X Y Z
Z Y X W V U T S R Q P O N M L K J I H G F E D C B A
```

"Now," she said, "we simply replace the letters on the top with the letters directly below each one: the ones in reverse."

She wrote out the cryptogram, and then using the cipher, decoded it directly below.

```
T L   G L   G S V   X O L X P N Z P V I
G O   T O   T H E   C L O C K M A K E R
```

Oona's blood began to course through her veins. "Deacon, what time does the clockmaker open his shop?"

"Mr. Altonburry?" Deacon asked. "Why, he has opened his shop at precisely eight o'clock every morning for the past thirty-five years."

Oona glanced at the clock on the wall. "Drat! I've slept in. It's eight o'clock now." She threw herself out of bed and began frantically dressing herself in the same dress she had worn the day before. "Isadora will already have the lead! Samuligan!"

Half a breath later a knock came at the door. "You called?"

"Tell Uncle Alexander that if he is coming to the tower events today we must leave at once!" she said urgently.

"The Wizard has been called away again this morning," Samuligan replied. "There has been an incident in the restaurant district. It seems one of the cooks has turned green all over, and has started sprouting tree branches from his fingers and roots from his toes. A sure sign of pixiewood poisoning. He sends his apologies, but he will once again be unable to accompany you."

Oona shook her head, unable to remember when her uncle had ever been so busy. Clearly, the enchanted objects and potions were becoming quite a problem. But there was no time to think too much about it.

"Get the carriage!" she said.

"No breakfast?" Samuligan inquired through the closed door. "I could whip up a nice crispy waffle, or some eggs, or perhaps a spot of coffee and some—"

Oona struggled with the buttons on the vest of her dress. "There's no time! She's managed to do it again, I'm sure of it."

"Who?" Samuligan asked.

"Isadora Iree!" Oona cried, throwing open the door and staring up at the faerie servant.

Samuligan grinned at her, showing more teeth than would have been humanly possible. "You look marvelous."

About to push past Samuligan, Oona suddenly stopped, realizing that the faerie servant had never complimented her in such a way. "Why, thank you," she said dubiously.

Behind her, Deacon burst into a caw of laughter.

Spinning around to see just what was so funny, Oona saw Deacon perched on the back of her dressing table chair. It took several seconds to see that, draped over the back of that same chair was her dress skirt. Looking down, Oona realized that she was wearing nothing but her petticoats.

"I understand it is the latest in modern fashion," said Samuligan. "It is all the rave in Europe."

Oona's face went beet red.

Thirty nail-biting minutes later, Oona stood fully dressed and slightly out of breath within the walls of the Dark Street Clock Shop.

"Yes indeed," said Mr. Altonburry, the master clock-maker, a thin, elderly gentleman with long gray hair and delicate hands nearly the same size as Oona's. Despite his age, he spoke with a hearty, youthful voice. "A young lady was in here before you. In fact, she was waiting at the door the moment I opened."

Oona glanced at the wall. Clocks of every shape and size ticked away the minutes and seconds, all of them running in perfect sync. Indeed, one of the benefits of living on Dark Street was the fact that all clocks ran in perfect syncopation with Pendulum House. From the clock towers at Dark Street Town Hall and Bradbury Church, to every pocket watch in every lapel pocket, they all moved together, without the slightest variance.

Oona sighed. "That means Isadora's already got a half-hour lead."

The clockmaker shrugged apologetically before handing Oona a bronze pendulum, about the size of her own hand. "That's true," he agreed, "but if you get a move on, you could catch up to the other young fellow."

The back of Oona's neck felt suddenly very cold. "You mean Roderick Rutherford was already here as well?"

"Left about five minutes before you came in," the clockmaker informed her.

Oona was out the door and sprinting toward the carriage before she heard Mr. Altonburry call after her. "Good luck!"

"Faster than you've ever driven!" Oona shouted to Samuligan, hurdling into her seat.

The whip cracked overhead, and ten harrowing

minutes later Oona could still hear the shouts of "Look out!" and "Watch where you're driving!" echoing through her head as she made her way up the stage steps in front of the tower, breathlessly handing the pendulum to the architect.

The crowd had dwindled to half of what had been there the day before. Her uncle was nowhere to be seen, but she could see Sir Baltimore at the front of the stage, running his hand nervously through his thick head of hair. Penelope sat at the edge of the stage, looking rather bored. Oona realized that, in her haste, she had forgotten to bring the book of faerie tales to return to the girl.

Deacon fluttered to the far end of the stage where he started up a conversation with Adler Iree, who, after finishing in fourth place the day before, would today be playing the part of a simple observer in the crowd. Oona met his gaze, and that same jittery feeling she'd experienced the day before filled her chest.

"Am I the last to arrive?" Oona asked the architect.

The architect nodded. "You'd better get a move on." He examined the pendulum before handing it back. "You'll want to hold on to that. You'll need it."

He gestured to a cage connected to a rope. "This will take you to the starting level," the architect said.

Oona stepped inside the cage, holding on to the frame and feeling quite unsafe as the rope pulled tight and began to lift her into the air. The higher she went, the more the wind began to play with the rickety elevator. The rope creaked unnervingly, along with the tower itself as the entire structure rocked slowly back and forth. Down below, the spectators began to look more and more like ants than people.

At last the elevator stopped, and Oona stepped gingerly from the box to a kind of ramshackle landing. She felt the wood dip significantly as she placed her weight upon it, and for one horrifying second she was certain the entire landing would tear away from the side of the building and she would go hurtling toward the ground. But the slight dip was as much as the landing moved, and Oona made her way briskly to the doorway in the side of the tower. With one last glance downward, she stepped into a large, high-ceilinged room filled with clocks.

The clocks sat upon bookshelves, countless levels of shelves that covered nearly every surface of the five-story-tall space. There were hundreds of shelves holding thousands of timepieces. It was like a library of clocks, with five levels of railed balconies skirting the outer walls. And yet upon entering the room, Oona immediately understood that something was wrong. Unlike every clock she had ever seen on Dark Street, each of these timepieces showed the incorrect time, the hour and minute hands pointing in all different directions.

A sign posted on an easel read:

WELCOME TO THE CLOCK FARM. HIDDEN
WITHIN EACH OF THESE DUMMY CLOCKS
ARE THREE *WORKING* CLOCKS. USE THE
PENDULUM GIVEN TO YOU BY THE
CLOCKMAKER TO ATTEMPT TO START
EACH ONE. FIND A WORKING CLOCK AND
YOU WILL RECEIVE YOUR KEY TO THE
EXIT. BUT BE CAREFUL. THERE ARE SOME
SURPRISES TO BE FOUND ALONG THE WAY.

Isadora Iree and Roderick Rutherford could be seen on the second-level balcony attempting to attach their pendulums to various clocks, and it quickly occurred to Oona that having arrived late was not such a bad thing after all. Assuming that Isadora and Roderick had started on the bottom floor, and were working their way up, then Oona could no doubt skip the entire first floor altogether, as all of those clocks had already been checked by the others.

Oona took to the ladder on the nearest wall and climbed past the second level, up to the third. She was just beginning to wonder about the part of the sign that had read, "There are some surprises to be found along the way," when a bell rang, and Isadora cried out from across the room.

Oona whirled around to discover that Isadora was no longer where she had been only a moment ago, but was shooting down a slide that had appeared beneath the second-story balcony. She came to a stop in a heap of skirts on the bottom floor, where she pounded her fist against the floorboards.

"That's the third trap I've hit!" she shouted in frustration.

"You should be more careful," Roderick called over his shoulder as he hooked his own pendulum onto the clock in front of him and attempted to give it a swing. He had hardly finished speaking his last word, however, when a bell rang and the clock popped open. A spring with a boxing glove mounted on the end uncoiled from inside and pounded Roderick twice in the head, driving him back against the balcony rail.

"Bloody hell!" Roderick cursed.

"Perhaps *you* should be more careful," Isadora said, her voice oozing with sarcasm as she pushed herself back to her feet on the bottom floor and quickly made her way back to the ladder. "This is all your fault, anyway! I should be done with this by now."

"And perhaps you should keep your mouth shut," Roderick said, shaking his head as if to clear it from seeing stars.

Trouble in paradise, Oona thought, and turned her

attention to the towering shelf of clocks before her, intent on blocking out Roderick and Isadora's squabble.

And yet, something that Isadora had said needled at her. Why was it Roderick's fault that Isadora was not finished with the challenge already? Looking at the task before them all—the enormity of the room, along with the sheer number of shelves, each groaning under the weight of all those clocks—it could take hours to find a working clock.

Especially with those traps, she thought nervously.

Why was it Roderick's fault that Isadora had not finished yet? . . . Unless . . .

Oona peered across the open room at Roderick, who was straightening himself against the handrail on the second floor and preparing to try another clock.

"It was you!" Oona shouted.

Both Roderick and Isadora froze. Roderick slowly turned around and peered back up at Oona, a quizzical expression on his handsome face.

"What was who?" he asked, though Oona thought she detected a hint of guilt in his voice.

Oona placed a hand on her hip. "It was you, Roderick, who stole the Punchbowl Oracle!"

"The punchbowl what?" Roderick asked. "Why would I steal a punchbowl?"

"You've been finding out the answers to the clues

ahead of time," Oona said. "You've been giving them to Isadora so she could gain the lead each day and win the challenges."

"I don't know what you're talking about," said Roderick.

"She's just a sore loser," Isadora said, now back on the second level. "And she wants to blame her own incompetence on my BOYFRIEND!"

"That's not true," Oona said. "You, Isadora, have been cheating."

Isadora smirked, then very coolly said: "Prove it."

"Is that a challenge?" Oona asked.

"It's whatever silly game you make of it," said Isadora.

Oona's resolve to win the competition suddenly burned inside of her. Isadora was right. Presently, there was no way to prove Isadora's guilt, but it *was* possible for Oona to beat her in the challenge today. That Oona could do.

She opened the clock in front of her, placed the pendulum on the hook, and then attempted to give it a swing. It didn't move. Clearly this was a nonworking clock. She did the same on the next three clocks. Nothing.

On the forth clock, the moment she placed the pendulum on the hook, a bell rang overhead. A spring beneath the floor released and sent Oona tumbling sideways down the balcony. She yelped in surprise, rolling to a stop some fifteen feet from where she had been standing.

Pushing herself back to her feet, she returned cautiously to the bookshelf she'd been working on and tried the next clock, hands shaking now, ready for something to happen. Nothing did. Just as she was preparing to place the pendulum on the next one, a loud gong rang from high above, and Oona cringed.

Isadora shouted. "*Yes!* I've got it. I've got a working one."

Oona turned. Sure enough, Isadora had found one of the three working clocks. Her pendulum was now swinging. The front door of the clock opened and a cuckoo bird popped out holding a key and a note in its mechanical mouth. Isadora unrolled the note and read aloud.

"Take this key to the top floor. The first one to unlock the door is the winner of today's challenge." She grinned maliciously up at Oona before snatching the key from the bird's mouth and running toward the ladder.

Oona could only shake her head. Isadora was going to win again, and there was nothing she could do to change it. She watched silently as Isadora climbed the ladder to the top of the room and disappeared from view. A moment later there was a click, followed by the sound of a door opening and closing.

Oona and Roderick locked eyes like a pair of gunfighters on a deserted town street. Something passed between them: a kind of frantic energy that Oona realized was something close to desperation. It was down to just the two of them. Only one of them would move on to the final challenge the following day with Isadora, and the race was truly on.

Oona hooked the pendulum onto the clocks, one after the other, moving relentlessly down the bookshelf along the third level. She could hear Roderick doing the same on the second floor below, and, with a feeling of sinking dread, Oona understood that it was now simply down to luck just as much as it was to how fast they could move.

Several minutes later, Oona was nearly done with the entire bookshelf she had started with, getting ready to begin the next one, when she placed the pendulum in the last clock on the bottom shelf.

The bell rang overhead and a second later she heard a click. She looked up just in time to find an entire bucket of water spill out of a hidden hatch and drench her from head to foot in icy cold water. Oona gasped for air, the chill biting into her skin as her dress absorbed the liquid like a sponge.

She blinked the water from her eyes, quickly rung out the bottom of her dress, and then moved on. It was just as she reached for the next clock that a bell rang out. Oona's heart skipped several beats, but it was Roderick who cried out in surprise. Oona spun around, only to discover Roderick hanging upside down, his ankles cinched together by a rope. Several seconds later the rope released him and he hit the ground hard enough to echo across the room.

As Roderick staggered back to his feet, Oona had another realization. It concerned the bell that rang every time a trap was sprung. Each time the bell rang, there was a brief period of time before the trap was actually activated.

She had a hunch that if she was quick enough, then she could potentially avoid any future traps if, instead of just waiting for the trap to do its darndest to her, she instead listened intently for the bell. The instant she heard it, she would jump out of the way. This, she decided, was a solid plan and worth a try.

With a feeling of jittery anticipation in her stomach, she placed the pendulum on the next hook. Nothing happened. Nothing happened on the clock after that either, nor the next. By the time she was through with half of the new bookshelf, she felt as if her nerves were on fire. More than once she thought she heard the beginning sounds of the bell and started to jump, only to realize she had simply imagined it.

It wasn't until the second to the last shelf that she was able to test her theory. Placing the pendulum on the middle clock—a heavy, baroque-style timepiece with ornate, gold-leaf designs—Oona heard the bell strike overhead and immediately jumped to one side. In almost the same instant, a hidden hatch popped open in the floor, revealing the very top of a slide—a slide that seemed to have popped out from beneath the balcony—that extended all the way to the bottom floor. Oona exhaled through pinched lips. She had just saved herself the trouble of having to climb all the way back up to the third floor.

She nodded decidedly, feeling quite relieved, as well as impressed with herself for having discovered the trick. She now had her strategy.

An hour later, Oona finished with the third floor, having avoided two boxing gloves on springs, three trapdoors, and a canister of glue and feathers, which, like the bucket of water, had spilled down from a compartment hidden in the balcony overhead.

Meanwhile, from the sound of it, Roderick had taken quite a beating down below. She was even beginning to feel somewhat sorry for him as she climbed the ladder to the fourth level, when, all of the sudden, a huge gong sound rang out from above.

"I got it!" Roderick shouted, and Oona's heart sank. Roderick had found one of the working clocks. That was it. It was all over. Roderick would be the next to reach the door, and Oona would be out of the contest completely.

She leaned over the rail on the fourth-floor balcony and peered down. Roderick had his key in hand and was beginning to climb the ladder. He looked horrible, drenched in water, one half of his jacket covered in a thick substance that Oona could only assume was glue, and a scattering of feathers sticking to the glue on his jacket and to the top of his head.

Oona turned from the railing, squeezing the palm-sized pendulum in her hand so hard that it hurt. She hated this feeling. Roderick was going to pass her up, just as Isadora had done, and there wasn't a single thing she could do about it. She walked to the nearest bookcase and jammed the pendulum down on the hook so hard she was certain that the clock would break.

The instant she slammed the pendulum into place another gong sounded overhead. A chill rolled down Oona's back, not from the cold damp of her sopping wet dress, but from the sudden rush of excitement. The clock-face opened and out came a cuckoo bird, just as it had with Isadora's clock, a note and key clasped in its beak.

Oona didn't hesitate. She snatched the key and leapt for the ladder, nearly colliding with Roderick. Her dress slapped him in the face as she scrambled up the ladder rungs. Roderick screamed like an animal, catching hold of her dress and yanking. Whether he had done it to catch his own balance, or out of spite, Oona didn't know, but her hands slipped. She felt herself beginning to fall backward, her arms swirling out at her sides.

Her foot jerked off its rung, kicking Roderick's hand.

His fingers released their grip and Oona fell forward, clasping the ladder with all her strength. Roderick slipped down two rungs before catching his own balance and once more beginning his assent.

Oona climbed.

Roderick was certainly a faster climber than she was, but there was no way for him to get past her. She reached the top balcony and heaved herself over the edge, looking quickly around for the exit. It seemed only a second had passed before Roderick was up as well. They both spotted the door at the same time, some ten yards away.

Oona had just begun to sprint, an electric, tingly sensation coursing through her veins, when she felt a hand on her back. Roderick shoved her from behind and she went down, hitting the floor with a heavy, wet smack. A moment later he was vaulting over her, shouting wildly, but his foot caught on her skirt. He fell forward with a cry of panic and surprise, toppling head over heals to the floor.

Oona didn't wait to see what would happen next. She catapulted off the floor and hurdled over Roderick's scrambling efforts to get back to his feet. She was past him in less than a second, her legs pumping furiously. Roderick cursed, rising hastily to his feet. He was just behind her, calling her this name and that, all semblance of chivalry gone.

Oona paid no mind. She threw herself at the door,

ramming her key into the lock and twisting in one fluid motion. At that moment nothing else existed, only the determination to get through that door first. To beat Roderick. To win. A second later and it was over.

Oona flung open the door and was greeted by the grinning face of the architect. She almost couldn't believe it.

She had done it! She had beat Roderick Rutherford, and she was going to the final challenge against Isadora Iree.

Her breath heaved in her chest, and a stitch ran down her side. Her hair was all in a tangle, and her wrist throbbed slightly from when she had taken her fall, yet Oona could neither remember ever seeing the sun shine so brightly, nor feeling such a sense of relief. It was a glorious day indeed.

CHAPTER FOURTEEN

The Tale of the Punchbowl Oracle

"I'm guessing you've made it into the top two," said the Wizard. He stood in the front yard, a pair of hedge clippers in hand. He was frowning at the rosebushes, as if unsure of what to do with them. Oona was surprised to find her uncle in the garden at all.

The Pendulum House front yard had grown quite untidy over the years. Trees sagged from the weight of overgrown limbs, and knots of thorny vines snaked through the tall weeds like ground cover in a rain forest. Just getting from the front gate to the front porch had become an obstacle course, with thorny barbs catching hold of Oona's dresses at every turn.

"Hello, Uncle," Oona said. "Samuligan mentioned

that you were called upon to deal with another case of pixiewood poisoning this morning."

He nodded. "And let's hope I've dealt with the last of it."

"To be sure. But this is the last place I'd expect to find you, Uncle. Why the sudden urge to garden?" Oona peered at the hedge clippers in his hand.

The Wizard shrugged. "Oh, I suppose it had something to do with seeing all of those branches and vines growing out of that cook's head. I managed to cure him, of course. He's already got his color back, and the branches have all but disappeared, but it just reminded me of what a sad state my own gardens were in." He waved his hand about the yard. "Someone needs to tidy up this mess."

"You could have Samuligan do it," Oona said. "He's just parking the carriage now."

The Wizard shook his head. "Of course I can, but where is the challenge in that?" He took in her haggard, soaking-wet attire. "Speaking of a challenge . . ."

Oona smiled at him. "Yes, Uncle. You guessed correctly. I am one of the top two. I have made it to the final challenge."

"Good for you," he said, then, raising a finger to one of the closed rosebuds, he uttered: *"Abra-ord-ion-all."*

The rosebud opened, showing its gorgeous red petals as they danced in the subtle breeze.

"Well done," said Deacon from Oona's shoulder.

"Hmm," Oona said. "That's a new spell."

The Wizard raised his eyebrows. "Actually, it's a very old spell. Quite obscure. In fact, it is one of the first non-conductor spells I ever learned."

"According to the *Encyclopedia Arcanna*," Deacon suddenly proclaimed, "roughly eighty-three percent of all known magic requires the use of a conductor such as a wand or staff through which the magic can be focused and aimed."

Oona shrugged, as if it all made very little difference to her. Her mind was too exhausted to be overly awed by a simple magic spell. There were other ways of getting a rose to open after all, she thought, such as trimming the overgrowth so that it actually received an ample amount of sunlight—no magic required. Still, she did not wish to ruin the moment for her uncle.

"My predecessor, Armand Flirtensnickle, taught it to me," her uncle said thoughtfully, "though I haven't used it in a very long time. Haven't even thought of that spell for years. Nearly forgot it altogether. I must have thought it was an insignificant spell that was good for nothing more than opening and closing a flower. Yet now, I wonder."

Oona stared up at her uncle, her arms hanging heavy at her sides. She hoped this would not turn into a long-winded lesson. What she wanted more than anything was to go upstairs and rest. But her uncle continued to look thoughtful, and as his apprentice she knew it would be impolite to interrupt.

The Wizard scratched at his bald head, the enormous structure of Pendulum House framing him from behind.

Four stories tall, with its numerous, interlocking roofs and the prow of a full-sized ship jutting from the second floor, the house towered above them in all of its magical glory. Five stories overhead, the ironwork weathervane rocked slowly in the warm breeze, and as she peered up at the numerous windows and various architectural details, Oona got the feeling, as she often did, that the ancient house was listening in on their conversation.

"I can remember Wizard Flirtensnickle teaching me that spell," the Wizard continued in a far-off sort of voice, as if he were traveling back in time to when he had been an apprentice. "I can remember the words he used to teach me its significance. He said that there are times when we humans open like a flower, our petals reaching outward for the answers we seek."

The Wizard once again tapped the rose with his finger.

"*Orx-ord-ion-ah*," he uttered: the counterspell.

The rose closed at once, its petals clamping shut so quickly that one of them detached, hovering briefly in the air before seesawing slowly to the ground.

"But often," he continued in that same thoughtful tone,

"the answers that we are looking for are on the inside, and no reaching outward is necessary."

He fell silent, and began pruning the thorny vines. Oona shook her head, wondering what on earth her uncle had been going on about . . . looking outside and inside? It sounded like a lot of nonsense to Oona, and she wondered briefly if her uncle was feeling all right.

Soreness and fatigue overtook her.

"Well, I'm very tired, Uncle," Oona said. "I think I'll head up and get out of this wet dress. Take a nap."

The Wizard nodded, but he pulled back from his cutting before uttering to himself: "On the inside." He peered attentively at the overgrown bushes like a sculptor contemplating a block of marble, and Oona made her escape.

Several minutes later she was empting the contents of her pockets onto her dressing table before wrestling out of the waterlogged dress. She slipped back into her nightgown, despite the earliness of the afternoon, and before long she was curled up in her bed, sound asleep.

Hours later, she awoke and peered blearily at the clock on the wall. It was nearly six o'clock.

She jerked up in bed. "Deacon!"

Her foot struck the book of faerie tales at her feet, sending it flying across the room. Deacon leapt into the air with a squawk of surprise.

"What? What is it?" he asked.

"You let me sleep the day away!"

Deacon landed on the bedpost. "I thought you deserved it. After all, there was no take-home clue for you to concentrate on."

Oona jumped to her feet and marched to the wardrobe, flinging it open. "Yes, Deacon, that is true, but there is still a mystery to be solved."

Once dressed, she stooped to pick up the book of faerie tales from the floor. It was as she straightened with the open book in her hand that Oona felt her breath leave her body and not return for several long seconds.

"What is it?" Deacon asked, instantly aware that something was not right.

Oona stared at the open book, at the page before her. She shook her head, trying to take in its meaning.

Deacon soared to her shoulder and peered down. There, on the left hand page, was the beginning of a story: an obscure faerie tale, according to the book's title. Deacon made a gasping sound before reading the title of the story.

"The Tale of the Punchbowl Oracle."

Oona said nothing, only continued to hold the book as she eased into her chair and began to read. Deacon read silently from her shoulder. Thirty minutes later Oona slammed the book shut and slapped it down on the dressing table, causing puffs of powder to plume up from an open canister.

Oona and Deacon sat in silence, absorbing what they had just read. Her hopes drained from her like water through a hole in a bucket.

Finally, Oona said: "The Punchbowl Oracle. It's nothing but a faerie tale."

Deacon nodded gravely. "And even in the story, it is nothing but a fictional creation. That cunning old farmer made it up in order to distract the hero from his true quest."

Oona nodded absently, recalling how the story had spoken of a young prince on his way to rescue a fair maiden. Trapped in a treacherous dragon's lair, the maiden would not have long to live, and so the prince raced to her aid. But the journey was long, and the night before he was to reach the dragon's lair, he knew he would need to rest. Fortunately for the prince, he came across an old farmer who offered him a place to sleep. The prince accepted gratefully.

That night over dinner, the farmer told the prince of his precious Punchbowl Oracle—a magical crystal bowl that could answer any question.

Naturally, the prince, who wished to know if he was going to succeed in conquering the dragon the next day, asked the farmer if he could see the punchbowl. But when the old farmer went to retrieve the mystical object, he discovered it had been lost.

"I must have left it somewhere on the farm," said the farmer. "But my memory is not what it use to be. I don't know where it is."

Since the farmer was old, and had bad knees, the prince offered to look for the bowl, partly because the old man seemed so upset about having lost it, and partly because the prince was nervous about fighting the dragon and wished to know the outcome ahead of time. For the next two days he searched the farm high and low, yet he found no sign of the bowl. Finally, on the third day, the prince decided that, bowl or no bowl, he had to be on his way to save the maiden fair. The prince graciously bid the old man farewell and rode his armor-clad steed to the top of the mountain where the terrible dragon was known to dwell.

"You have arrived too late." The dragon laughed. "I have already eaten your precious lady. Had you not stayed so long with the old man, you might have saved her."

"How do you know about the old man?" asked the prince, horrified that he had arrived too late.

"Because the old man is a friend of mine," said the dragon. "There is no Punchbowl Oracle, you fool. It was just a lie to distract you from your quest. You silly princes . . . you fall for it every time."

The story had ended on a rather gruesome note, with the dragon gobbling up the bereft prince, and then flying to the old man's house, where the two of them played a game of dominoes and laughed about the whole thing. Oona could see why it was such an obscure faerie tale. Who, besides that strange little Penelope Rutherford, would wish to hear such a dreary tale before bedtime?

The popularity of the story, however, was presently the least of Oona's worries. The realization that she had been fooled hit her hard, along with the understanding that if the gypsy woman had lied about the bowl, then it was likely she had lied about having the so-called "sight." Her hint that Oona was not responsible for the burden she held was nothing more than a faerie tale in and of itself.

Oona was enraged.

"We must find Madame Romania from Romania at once!" she said vehemently. She was on her feet and reaching for the door. "We need to find out why she made up this business with the punchbowl."

Deacon ruffled his feathers. "We do indeed."

Madame Romania from Romania did not answer her door. Oona knocked several more times on the back of the caravan, but to no avail. The shadows from the trees stretched out like groping hands in the failing light.

"That's two days in a row she has not been in. It would appear that Madame Romania from Romania has abandoned her caravan, Deacon. What do you say to having a little look inside?"

"Are you sure that is a wise idea?" Deacon asked, glancing nervously around.

Evening was creeping in, and the park appeared deserted. Doing her best to appear casual, like someone simply out for an evening stroll and admiring the caravan's decorations, Oona walked around the side of the wagon and stopped to read the sign painted along the side.

MADAME ROMANIA FROM ROMANIA! FORTUNES TOLD, PALMS READ, SECRETS REVEALED INSIDE!

"Hmm," she intoned. "You know, Deacon, the first time I saw that sign I noticed how new it looked. As if it had been freshly painted."

Deacon glanced over the sign and nodded. "Now that you have drawn my attention to it . . . you are quite right. The sign does appear to be in excellent condition, if compared to the rest of the caravan."

Oona shot a quick glance over her shoulder and then hurriedly scooted beneath the wagon. Deacon hopped to the ground and watched Oona flip the latch on the underside of the caravan. The trapdoor swung open on its hinges.

"Fairly easy, I'd say," Oona said, and poked her head inside.

The inner wagon was black as pitch, and not at all inviting, but Oona pulled herself inside. Something pricked her finger as she seated herself on the edge of the trapdoor.

"Ouch," she said.

"Are you all right?" Deacon asked from below.

"I think so," she said, and produced a match from her pocket. She struck it against the edge of the trapdoor, and the fabric-lined room filled with flickering light. An oil lamp sat on a nearby shelf, and Oona lit it, turning the dial to full.

The silver charms that hung from the ceiling glistened eerily in the lamplight, and a sudden panicky feeling stole over her at the thought of being caught. She did her best to ignore the fear.

Deacon hopped inside. "What is it you are looking for?"

Oona tore aside the curtain that divided the front of the caravan from the back, revealing row after row of hanging garments, all jam-packed together, tighter even than Isadora Iree's wardrobe.

Oona held the lamp up. "Costumes."

"Costumes?" Deacon said. "There must be—"

"Thousands," Oona said.

"But what does it mean?" Deacon asked.

Oona dropped to the floor and felt around the spot near the trapdoor. Several seconds later she held up a long quill.

"Here," she said. "I pricked my hand on this when I first entered."

"A porcupine quill?" Deacon asked.

Oona nodded. "And who do we know, Deacon, that would need thousands of costumes, and is also in the habit of keeping porcupines as pets?"

"You don't mean that Madame Romania from Romania is actually the Master of Ten Thousand Faces? Albert Pancake?"

"I mean precisely that, Deacon," Oona said. "That is why there is a trapdoor in the middle of the wagon. This is the same type of wagon used by theater troupes around the world. The walls can be pulled open, and the floor becomes a stage."

Deacon hopped to the tabletop. "I see. The trapdoor is used to create certain special effects during a show and would be very handy in a quick-change performance. But why would Albert Pancake wish to tell you such an outrageous story?"

"I have my suspicions," Oona said. "But I think we should ask *him* that very question. Come, Deacon." She turned down the oil lamp until it went out completely, and then lowered herself through the trapdoor. "I believe tonight is a perfect night for the theater."

CHAPTER FIFTEEN

The Theater

The theater was packed. When Oona inquired about tickets at the box office, she was turned away when the attendant pointed to the sign in the window.

SOLD OUT!

Oona wasn't too discouraged, however. As many of the theatergoers were entering the building, she casually merged into the meandering line and slipped inside quite unnoticed, despite being the only girl in line with a raven on her shoulder.

Ushers stood guard at each of the auditorium doors, ready to check tickets and escort the audience to their seats. With no ticket, Oona knew she would need to find another way in. A door at the far end of the lobby caught her attention. Navigating her way through the crowd of richly dressed patrons, she soon saw that the door was marked with the letters: BSL.

"BSL?" said Deacon. "What does it mean?"

"My guess is that it stands for 'backstage left,'" Oona said, and, glancing anxiously over her shoulder to see that no one was watching, she turned the knob and slipped inside. It took several seconds for her eyes to adjust to the dim light. She peered curiously around. The two of them had entered what appeared to be a long, dark corridor.

"So this must lead backstage," Deacon said.

Oona could only hope he was correct. She had never been backstage in the theater before, and she was fascinated. More than her curiosity to see how a theater worked, however, it was her determination to discover why Albert Pancake had deceived her that propelled her forward.

The two of them slowly made their way down the narrow passageway. Oona tripped once on a stray sandbag, nearly losing her balance completely, and then shortly afterward she tumbled headlong into a pile of rope.

"Are you injured?" Deacon asked concernedly from beside her.

Oona pushed herself back to her feet. "I hit my knee,

but I'm fine. This theater life is more dangerous than I would have thought."

Deacon chuckled as they pressed forward, but Oona didn't find it very funny. She had knocked her knee quite hard and limped the rest of the way down the narrow hallway.

At last, they exited the corridor and found themselves in the backstage wing of the theater. Long swaths of black fabric hung from the ceiling high overhead, keeping the theatergoers from seeing backstage. Oona could hear the audience taking their seats, hundreds of voices chattering away.

"Can I help you?" a voice asked.

Oona spun around to see a man leaning against a line of ropes, his arms crossing his broad chest and a toothpick sticking from the corner of his mouth.

"Oh, hello," Oona said, throwing her hand to her chest. "You startled me."

"You ain't supposed to be back here," said the man. His face was cast in shadow, though by the bulgy arms that stretched out his shirtsleeves, Oona took him to be someone who worked backstage, a stagehand.

"I am looking for Mr. Pancake," Oona said. Her voice trembled slightly from being startled, and she suddenly felt very silly.

"Mr. Pancake is getting ready to perform, love," the

stagehand said. "If you have a ticket, then you can watch him out there, with the rest of the audience."

"But . . . it is a matter of life and death," Oona lied. "I must speak with him before the performance."

The stagehand stepped forward. Oona stiffened as he uncrossed his bulky arms, placing his hands on his hips. Oona's nerves returned in full force as he leaned down, his face coming within an inch of hers. She could smell his breath, which smelled overpoweringly of mint. "You can give the message to me, love. I'll get it to him. You can trust me."

The man's face was still shrouded in the darkness of backstage, yet his eyes caught the light. They sparkled, and Oona cocked her head to one side, as if noticing something.

"Please keep your distance, sir," Deacon said, puffing himself up menacingly on Oona's shoulder.

The man took no notice and did not retreat. The stench of mint enshrouded him. "Just give the message to me, missy. I'll get it to him. And hurry it up. We got a show to put on here."

"I'm afraid that isn't possible," Oona said.

"What isn't possible?" asked the stagehand.

"For you to give the message to Mr. Pancake," Oona said. "Unless you give the message to yourself."

The stagehand's head snapped back, eyes blinking. "What?"

"You are Albert Pancake," Oona said. "The Master of Ten Thousand Faces. I recognize you."

The stagehand stood up straight. "That's impossible. How? I mean, um, you're wrong. I'm just a stagehand. Work backstage, love."

He flexed his arm, as if this might prove his identity.

"I recognize your eyes," Oona said. "You are very good, Mr. Pancake. Exceptional. But the one thing you cannot change about yourself is your eyes; I noticed that very thing about you yesterday, during our meeting in the lobby, when you imitated my uncle. You looked just like him . . . all except for the eyes. But it wasn't until I saw you in the dark tonight, without the rest of your miraculous face to distract me, that I realized I had seen those eyes before. I am speaking, of course, of Madame Romania from Romania's eyes, whose face was hidden behind that ragged cloth. That, combined with the smell of mint, which you seem to be so fond of chewing, gave you away."

For a long moment, the stagehand only stood there, his face enshrouded in shadow, and yet Oona could see those eyes first round in surprise, and then begin to shake back and forth in obvious disbelief.

At last he said: "That's incredible. In all my years as a performer, never once has anyone seen through my disguise."

He sat on the floor, and hung his head forward.

"And now, Mr. Pancake," Oona said, "I must ask you why you masqueraded yourself as a gypsy woman and told me that dreadful lie about the Punchbowl Oracle?"

Albert Pancake did not look up, but only continued to sit in the darkened wings of the theater. The sounds of the audience drifted in through the stage wings.

"I was hired to do it," Mr. Pancake said in a small voice. "I was told exactly what to do: the portrayal of the gypsy woman, the punchbowl, and, most specifically, to say the line, 'You are not responsible for the burden you hold.' I was to convince you of the bowl's existence and then discover its theft while in your presence. If I accepted the job, I would receive a large sum of money. More money than I could resist for such a simple job, really."

"Who put you up to it?" Oona demanded. "Tell me the truth and I will promise not to tell the police."

Mr. Pancake suddenly looked up. "The police? What did I do wrong? I simply impersonated an old woman and told some fortunes. There are no laws against it."

Oona thought this over for a moment. It was true. No laws had been broken. None that she could think of, anyway. And indeed, she realized that if anyone deserved punishment, it was herself, for being so gullible in the first place. She should have known better, should have listened to both Deacon and her uncle. But the idea of being relieved of her guilt had overridden her clearheadedness.

"Who hired you to distract me with this wild-goose chase, Mr. Pancake?" Oona demanded, unable to hide her anger. She leaned forward, peering down at the sitting man in the same menacing manner he had done to her only minutes before. "Whoever put you up to it most likely wished for me to focus my energies on this hopeless mystery instead of on the contest," she said. "Let me guess. Was it Isadora Iree?"

Mr. Pancake shook his head.

"No?" Oona said. "Then perhaps it was her mother, Madame Iree?"

Again the Master of Ten Thousand Faces shook his head.

"Who then? Roderick?" she asked. "Or maybe . . ."

She trailed off, the realization coming to her slowly. She slapped her forehead. "Why did I not see it immediately? Sir Baltimore. He hired you to distract me with the story, the same story that he read time and time again to his daughter from her book of obscure faerie tales. Deacon, do you remember Adler Iree saying that Sir Baltimore had bet a substantial amount of money on the contest?"

Deacon clacked his beak before saying: "Sir Baltimore knew that you were the most able-minded challenger. He hired Mr. Pancake to distract you with all this poppycock of magic bowls so that his son, Roderick, could take the lead."

Mr. Pancake pushed himself up from the floor and sighed deeply. "Well, it would seem you have figured everything out for yourself, and so, if you are quite done—"

He made as if to move past Oona toward the stage.

"Just a moment," Oona said, stepping in front of him. "I haven't figured out everything. For instance, the ring."

Mr. Pancake's brow rose, and Oona could tell that he knew precisely what ring she was speaking of. "You mean the dressmaker's ring?" he said. "You found it, did you? Baltimore said you would be clever. Well, seeing as the cat is out of the bag, I'll tell you. The ring was my doing, but not completely my idea."

"How so?" Oona asked.

"Well, the dressmaker—Madame Iree—came into my caravan early on during the party and wished to have her palm read. It was not the first time I had played the role of Madame Romania from Romania, and I am quite good at telling fortunes."

Oona folded her arms. "*False* fortunes."

Mr. Pancake shrugged, raising his hands in a what-can-I-say gesture. "False is my game, Miss Crate. So anyway, I asked Madame Iree to close her eyes . . . and . . . well, let's just say that the ring slipped from her finger."

Mr. Pancake wiggled his own fingers, as if to show how easily a ring might slip off by itself. Oona shook her head, disbelieving. Mr. Pancake had clearly stolen it. "At any rate," he continued, with a clearing of his throat, "once she had departed, I dropped the ring through the caravan's trapdoor."

Oona nodded, a look of both understanding and annoyance crossing her face. "So you took the ring and dropped it beneath the caravan to leave a false trail . . . in case any one, such as myself, should go looking around for clues."

Mr. Pancake shrugged. "It was all Baltimore's idea. He suggested that I plant some evidence. Told me to take something from one of the guests and leave it somewhere that was not too obvious. Something that would keep you busy looking in the wrong direction. I thought that was going a bit overboard, but he seemed to be under the impression that you would be curious enough to find it. He said that if you were anything like your father, that you would stop at nothing to solve such a mystery. He was banking on it."

"And he was right," Oona said, not without a pinch of pride.

"Now, if you will excuse me," Mr. Pancake said rather hurriedly, "my audience awaits."

The man pushed Oona aside and sauntered through

the swaths of long, black fabric and onto the stage. The auditorium filled with the sound of applause. He grinned broadly, waving to the audience as he began: "Ladies and gentlemen. Welcome one and all . . ."

Oona stared after him, unable to listen, thinking instead about what she had just learned. It all made a perfect kind of sense . . . and yet . . .

"And yet, that still does not explain how Isadora is getting all of the answers to the challenges," she said, and could not help but feel a sort of anticlimactic sense of accomplishment at having solved one mystery, only to be confronted straightaway by yet another.

Gloomily, Oona made her way back through the darkened corridor to the front of the theater. They found Samuligan waiting for them at the curb. The carriage ride home was a cold one. The temperature outside had dropped considerably, and with a glance through the window toward the sky, Oona wondered if they were in store for some rain.

"Fitting," she said.

"I beg your pardon?" said Deacon.

Oona only shook her head despondently as the carriage rolled past Oswald Park. A dampness filled the air, and the park appeared dark and abandoned. The shadowy form of the tower could be seen jutting from the center of the park like a crooked finger that pointed to some hidden message in the sky. But the sky was black, its meaning obscured by the swirl of accumulating clouds.

As the tower disappeared from view, Oona leaned heavily against the window and sighed. The mystery was a blur, and it irked her to no end. Try as she might, she simply could not understand how Isadora was doing it.

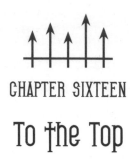

CHAPTER SIXTEEN

To the Top

On the following day, the Wizard escorted Oona to the park. "Wouldn't want to miss the final challenge," he said. "In all the years the contest has existed, no one has managed to beat the final task."

Oona nodded, her gaze fixed out the carriage window, focusing on nothing in particular as they rolled down the nearly deserted street. The sky was gray, and rain beat on the roof, coming down in heavy sheets. There was a chill in the air, and yet Oona hardly noticed her own discomfort.

It was one needling thought that absorbed her, one exasperating question that blocked out her surroundings like a thick curtain. How was Isadora Iree getting the answers to the clues ahead of time? It was simply infuriating. Half the night she had pondered the question and had been unable to find a satisfactory answer.

"There is simply not enough information," Oona said.

"What was that?" the Wizard asked.

"Hmm?" said Oona. "Oh, nothing."

"Is something bothering you, my dear?" the Wizard asked. "I would think you might be excited to have gotten as far as you have in the competition. But you look as if you've lost your best friend."

Oona nodded, but said nothing. She, of course, had lost something. Something precious indeed. She'd lost the hope that her mother and sister had died for some reason other than her own magical incompetence.

She thought of Sir Baltimore, and how he had set the whole thing up, how clever he had been to have the gypsy woman hint that Oona was not responsible for the burden she held. Now that she thought about it, the words could have applied to most anyone, and most anything. Sir Baltimore knew of the accident in Oona's past—it was common knowledge, after all—and so he had created the perfect phrase to capture her attention: "You are not responsible for the burden you hold!"

How vague and enticing the promise had been. And then the hint that only the punchbowl could tell the truth of the matter. Despite the fact that her uncle had assured her on countless occasions that she should not blame herself for what had happened, she had always known that those were just words to comfort her. It had been she who had conjured the Lights of Wonder, and she alone who had lost control.

But then came the gypsy's prediction, and she'd found tremendous hope in the idea that the punchbowl might show her the truth; let her see what happened with her own eyes.

Now that possibility was gone.

The carriage creaked to a stop. Samuligan hopped down from the driver's seat and opened the compartment door. Oona stepped down to find that, regardless of the heavy downpour, she remained perfectly dry, as if an invisible umbrella were protecting her and Deacon. The Wizard stepped from the compartment and glanced at the magical canopy, nodding approvingly.

"Excellent idea," he told Samuligan. "No sense getting drenched."

"I thought you would approve," said Samuligan, and the four of them made their way to the center of the park, where the rain pounded against the tower's uneven sides, making it look more unsteady than ever. Toward the top, the tower swayed in the high wind like a living thing.

At the front of the stage stood a scattering of spectators, though nowhere as many as on the first or even second day of the contest. The rain had kept them all home, though there were a few familiar faces at the foot of the stage. Madame Iree and Headmistress Duvet stood together, huddled beneath their enormous umbrellas.

Several feet away, Adler Iree stood, hands in pockets, no umbrella to speak of, looking highly amused. Why he would wish to stand in the soaking rain like that was beyond Oona. Boys could be so strange sometimes. Yet he gave her a thumbs-up gesture as she took to the stage, and she felt her heart skip a beat. It was the first positive feeling she'd felt all morning. But that burst of delight was quickly smashed when she caught sight of Roderick Rutherford and his father.

Oona forced herself to look away, fearing that she might march straight across the stage and slap Sir Baltimore in the face. But she appeased herself with the thought that Roderick had not made it to the final challenge. It was now down to just Oona and Isadora—Isadora, who was presently holding an umbrella and standing beside a large hand-painted sign. The architect was nowhere to be seen.

Oona moved to Isadora's side, reading the sign:

BOTH CONTESTANTS ARE TO TAKE THE ELEVATOR
TO THE TOP FLOOR FOR THE FINAL CLUE.

Oona and Isadora looked at the rickety elevator and then at each other.

"Ready to lose?" Isadora asked.

"Easy," Deacon whispered in Oona's ear.

Oona cracked a smile. "I will see you when I return, Deacon."

Deacon dipped his head before flying from her shoulder to wait beside the Wizard and Samuligan. Oona and Isadora stepped into the elevator cage and were immediately hoisted into the air. As they rose, Samuligan's invisible umbrella disappeared, leaving Oona open to the rain.

Isadora let out a sharp laugh, but a moment later, a strong wind gusted, tearing Isadora's umbrella from her hand. The umbrella folded itself and fell earthbound through the bars of the elevator cage. A bark of laughter could be heard coming from below, and Oona recognized it instantly to be Samuligan's sharp chortle.

"You did that!" Isadora snapped.

"I did nothing of the sort!" Oona snapped back.

Isadora shook her head, disbelieving. "I know you can do all kinds of magic. And still you can't beat me in this contest."

"The reason I haven't beat you is because you've been cheating," Oona said.

The two of them were getting plenty soaked, and the higher they went, the harder the wind began to blow.

Isadora clung to the metal cage of the elevator, her wet

hair slapping against her forehead. "Like I said before . . . prove it!"

"I will prove it, Isadora," Oona said, driblets of water rolling down her cheeks. "Just as soon as I beat you in this competition."

"No chance," said Isadora.

"We'll see," said Oona, and the two of them were quiet for what seemed a long time.

The elevator continued to climb, rocking from side to side in the increasingly strong winds. The rain pelted them, soaking their dresses through to the skin, and by the time they reached the top, the two of them were shivering, hands clinging to the bars of the elevator cage for support.

Oona glanced down. She could barely make out the stage through the rain as the tower rocked several feet from one side to the other, like a ship adrift in unsteady waters.

Feeling slightly dizzy, not to mention queasy in the stomach, Oona looked away from the ground and up toward the top of the pyramid. The point disappeared in the thick soup of clouds overhead.

A metal landing with a rail along one side jutted six feet out of the side of the pyramid like a wobbly dock. Water poured off the metal in a smooth torrent. It looked quite slick.

"We should go one at a time," Oona suggested.

Isadora nodded, though, from the look on her face, Oona could see that the fine young lady had lost much of her confidence.

"Would you like me to go first?" Oona asked.

Isadora shook her head. "No. I was the first to finish yesterday. I should be the first to enter the pyramid."

Oona raised an eyebrow and shrugged. She looked at the slippery walkway and then down to the blurry outline of the park hundreds of feet below.

"Be my guest," she said.

But Isadora did not move, only continued to stare at the metal walkway as if it were a vicious creature waiting for her to step into its lair.

Finally, Oona moved forward.

"One of us has to go first," she said, and stepped gingerly from the elevator to the landing, grabbing hold of the railing along the left side.

The landing dipped and creaked, but held. So long as she kept hold of the railing, she thought she would be okay. Slowly, she began sliding her feet across the metal walkway. The landing creaked and squeaked like a wounded animal in the rain, but the closer she came to the pyramid, the more confident she began to feel.

Without warning, the walkway suddenly pitched back, and Oona's feet slid out from beneath her. Her scream cut through the rain like a knife as she clung desperately to the railing. For one terrifying instant it seemed like the entire landing was going to tear away from the building, but the movement stopped and Oona quickly pulled herself back to her feet. A second scream pierced the storm. Whipping her head around, Oona saw why the landing had pitched back.

Isadora Iree was hanging off the end of the landing, feet dangling over the edge. She clung to the bottom of the railing, wailing in terror.

"Help! Help! I'm going to fall!"

Unthinking, Oona darted back. She thrust her hand out and clasped Isadora's fingers. Isadora clamped down on Oona's hand, and Oona heaved back with all of her strength. Isadora's soaked dress did not help. She was terribly heavy.

Oona's feet started to slip, and for one heart-stopping instant she was quite certain that the two of them were going to tumble over the edge together. Isadora kicked her legs, as if trying to swim through the rain back onto the landing. It seemed to work.

One hand on the railing and the other clamped to both of Isadora's, Oona let loose a low grunt and tugged with everything she had. Isadora slid across the lip of the landing just as Oona's hand slipped. Oona toppled backward and caught hold of the railing. Her breath stopped. She righted herself and looked around, fully expecting to see Isadora gone.

But Isadora was there, coughing and pulling herself up on the railing. Oona breathed a sigh of relief before gingerly making her way to the door in the side of the pyramid. Several seconds later Isadora joined her, the two of them shivering like skeletons in an earthquake.

"Th-th-thank you," said Isadora, the words sounding genuine, yet foreign upon her lips.

"Of course," Oona said, feeling relieved that she had saved Isadora's life, and yet another part of her—the competitive part—felt nervous and uneasy about what they were about to face.

This was the final stage of the competition, after all—the part that no one had ever completed—and it was with both excitement and trepidation that she swallowed a heavy lump in her throat, and said: "Let's get this thing started."

She opened the door, and the two of them entered the final stage of the Magician's Tower Contest.

CHAPTER SEVENTEEN

The Final Challenge

The architect was waiting for them at the center of the empty pyramid.

A fire crackled within a large brick fireplace, and the room was quite warm. Aside from the fireplace, the only other adornment was that of a metal chain that hung down from the center point of the pyramid. The chain stopped approximately ten feet above the floor, at the end of which hung a black box. About the size of a bread box, the mysterious object dangled directly above a large red X painted on the floor.

The two girls approached the tiny man in the top hat, and Oona eyed the box wondrously. This was it, she knew: the infamous black puzzle box, the one she had read about and which no contestant had ever managed to solve. She was eager to get her hands on it.

Static electricity suddenly filled the room, and a heartbeat later, thunder boomed outside as if a giant fist had pounded the top of the tower.

Oona and Isadora jumped.

"Congratulations," said the architect. "You are the final two contestants. You have made it through many trials to get here, and you both deserve a hearty round of applause."

The architect began to clap loudly as Oona and Isadora stopped several feet from the center of the room. They looked at each other, no doubt sharing the same sense of embarrassment at being applauded by a single person, and yet the rain on the walls created a kind of auditory illusion, as if thousands of invisible people filled the room, applauding in a raucous standing ovation.

This went on for far too long, in Oona's opinion, but finally the odd little man stopped clapping and steepled his hands at his chest. His expression became quite serious.

"I have only one question for you now," he said. "One final, mental feat. Answer correctly and you will move on to the final physical challenge, a task that no one has conquered in over five hundred years. Answer incorrectly and you will be out of the competition." He smiled, spreading his hands in a grand gesture like a circus ringleader. "We will flip a coin to see which of you will attempt to answer first."

Oona's eyebrows pulled closer together. "But if the first person answers correctly, then won't the second person have the advantage of giving the same answer?"

The architect touched the side of his nose and nodded. "That is precisely the case. If that happens, we will then flip another coin to see which of you will have the first hour with the final challenge." His eyes flicked toward the hanging box. "Now, Miss Iree, since you won the challenge yesterday, I will allow you to call the toss. If your side lands faceup, then you will go first."

The architect removed a coin from his pocket and tossed it keenly into the air.

"Heads," Isadora called. The coin flipped end over end, arching high, nearly hitting the hanging black box. It landed in the middle of the red X on the floor.

"Heads it is!" declared the architect.

Oona breathed a sigh of relief, realizing that any advantage Isadora might have had—like knowing the answer ahead of time—was about to become Oona's own advantage.

"Please step forward, Miss Iree," said the architect, indicating that she should stand in the center of the red X.

Isadora took her place, facing the architect, look-ing calm and collected. Oona noticed a slight smirk on

Isadora's face. The girl was so infuriatingly sure of herself!

"Are you ready?" the architect asked.

"As ever," said Isadora.

"Very good then. My question is this: What time do the Iron Gates open upon New York City?"

Oona's mouth dropped open and she shook her head, unsure if she should believe her own ears. This was the final mental challenge? After all they had been through? Could it possibly be that easy? She forced herself to hold back a laugh. It was ridiculous, and yet . . . and yet to look at Isadora Iree, one might have thought the architect had asked her to calculate the distance between the earth and the moon using only a hand ruler.

At first, Oona mistook Isadora's dismay for that of surprise at the simplicity of the question, but it did not take long to realize that Isadora, for whatever reason, was simply stumped. Her eyes rounded, shifting nervously in their sockets.

Finally, Isadora took in a deep breath and uttered the word: *"Rutabaga."*

Oona took in a sharp breath, unable to believe her ears. Had Isadora Iree just said *rutabaga*?

Even more peculiar, the architect was presently nodding his head, as if, yes indeed, the answer to his question was the name of a root vegetable. Oona had never felt more confused in her life.

"I thought you might say that," the architect said. "But I'm sorry, Miss Iree, your answer is incorrect."

"Oh, I know," Isadora said quickly. "I know it is, but . . . well . . . the real answer is—"

But what the real answer was, Isadora did not get the chance to say. She let out a sudden yelp as a trapdoor gave way beneath her feet, and the fine young lady disappeared through the hole below. A moment later, the door closed, once again displaying the large red X on the floor, and leaving Oona and the architect alone.

"Oh, dear," said the architect. "I forgot to get my coin back."

"Is she going to be okay?" Oona asked.

"She'll be fine," said the architect. "In fact, she'll most likely be coming out at the bottom of the tower"—he glanced at his pocket watch—"right about . . . now. It is the longest slide I have ever designed . . . quite fun."

Oona had an idea that Isadora Iree would not be having fun on her way down, but she kept this thought to herself as the architect motioned for her to step forward onto the X, and Oona's nerves all at once began to tingle.

"Your turn, Miss Crate," the architect said. "My question to you is: What time do the Iron Gates open upon New York City?"

Oona hesitated, running the question over in her mind, making sure there were no tricks. The architect's eyebrows rose, as if surprised at her hesitation, and Oona felt quite silly. What had Isadora been thinking—*rutabaga?*—when the real answer was without any doubt . . .

"Midnight?" She said it questioningly, as if she were unsure, and then closed her eyes, half expecting the floor to fall out from beneath her. The floor, however, did not move. Several seconds later, Oona opened her eyes to find the architect looking rather amused.

"Of course midnight is correct," he said. "When has it ever been different?"

Oona felt her breath leave her lungs, suddenly aware that she had been holding it.

"Congratulations," the architect said. "You have made it to the final challenge, and you have done it honestly." The short man burst out laughing, shaking his head back and forth. "Rutabaga! I can't believe she actually said it."

Oona laughed as well, though she suspected they were not laughing at the same thing. Finally, she asked: "How did you know she would say rutabaga?"

The architect composed himself, clearing his throat and straightening his hat. "It was in the plans," he said. "Rutabaga was the answer to the final question, but it was a false answer, meant to expose anyone who might have gotten their hands on the plans and used them to cheat."

Oona placed her finger to her lips, thinking. So that was it. Isadora had gotten her hands on the plans, and that was how she had been winning all the tasks—not from some all-knowing punchbowl after all.

"But how did Isadora get hold of the plans?" Oona asked.

"That, I don't know," the architect said. "The only time I was ever separated from the plans was the night of the party. But the plans were missing for only a minute or two before they were found on the ground."

Oona nodded. "Then how did she get hold of them?"

The architect once again shrugged. "It does not matter now. And you have one final test to complete." He gestured toward the hanging box overhead. "I submit to you: the box."

He pulled at what appeared to be some kind of hidden lever along the wall, and the box dropped from the chain. Oona took in a sharp breath, catching it in her open arms. It was very light and extremely smooth. The black color seemed to come from the wood itself, rather than from paint or a stain. Rolling it over in her hands, she could find nowhere to open it. No lock. No seam. No hinge. Nothing but solid box. It was a perfect mystery, and Oona was fascinated.

The architect tapped the box with a short, stubby finger. "In over five hundred years of these contests, the best and the brightest of minds have come to this very place and held that box. None of them have managed to open it. Perhaps you will be the one." He looked at his watch. "You have one hour."

As usual, when Oona had a problem before her, she barely heard the words spoken to her. She moved to the fireplace, where the light was best and the warmth might begin to dry her soaking dress and wet hair. She sat on the floor before the hearth, the box cradled in her lap.

At first she only looked at it, as if her gaze might penetrate the box, discovering its contents by willpower alone, but after a minute of heavy concentration she began to run the tips of her fingers along the sides of the smooth surface.

She found no flaw. No cracks. Nothing to indicate that it could be opened at all. She shook it beside her ear, like a child attempting to discover the contents of a birthday present.

She reached into her pocket for her magnifying glass, only to discover that it was not there. She checked all of her pockets, but they were empty. To her dismay, she all at once remembered changing out of her wet dress the day before. She had placed the contents of her pockets—including the magnifying glass—on her dressing table and then gone straight to bed, evidently failing to place them in the fresh dress she put on when she awoke.

She sighed. It might have been helpful to have had the

glass, even if it had been just the comfort of having a bit of her father with her . . . to help her see clearly.

Systematically, she applied pressure to the corners of the box with her thumbs.

More than half an hour passed, and the front half of her dress began to dry. Tendrils of steam rose off the fabric, spiraling into the upper reaches of the pyramid in swirling, chaotic patterns that broke apart and rejoined like misty puzzle pieces. Oona placed the box on the floor in front of her and stood on it. She jumped up and down. Nothing. She stepped from the box and watched its immaculate surface flicker in the firelight, as if it were an animal that might at any moment make a sudden dash for the door.

The tower continued to sway in the storm, and the rain seemed to fall even harder. Thunder cracked over-head. The tower trembled, yet Oona remained oblivious to her surroundings.

It was as if nothing else in the world existed, save for the puzzle before her, and it was as she stared fixedly at the box, its shinny black surface flickering in the orange fire glow, that the idea came to her. It seemed so simple. *Too* simple, perhaps, but all the same . . . she picked the box up, and then, before she could think twice about what she was doing, she tossed it into the fire.

Half expecting the architect to protest, she glanced

over her shoulder, but the tiny man in the tall hat, who was waiting patiently in his place at the center of the room, remained as quiet as snowfall.

By now the fire had burned down to mostly red-hot embers. Surely the box would instantly catch fire, and hopefully, if her hunch was correct, crack open from the heat. The box landed on the embers with a dazzling spray of sparks, several of which sizzled out on Oona's damp dress. She brushed them away with the back of her hand and waited for something to happen.

Nothing. Not only did the box *not* catch fire, it did not so much as begin to smoke. Again, Oona watched the box, waiting. One minute. Three minutes. When five minutes had passed, Oona reached out a tentative hand and felt the top of the box, which remained cool to the touch.

"Remarkable," she said, and pulled the box from the fire, amazed at how the object managed to maintain a steady temperature, no matter what its environment— yet truthfully, when she thought about it, she was not amazed at all. Was this not the very sort of thing she had been learning about for the past five years? It was indeed. This was no logic puzzle, no comprehensible riddle. It was nothing the mind could grasp at all. This box was undeniably . . .

"Magic," she said.

It came out sounding as if she should have known

it all the time; as if it were some inevitable element in her life that she could not get away from. Deny it all she wanted, magic was a part of her world, and perhaps even more so, it was a part of *her*. Indeed, it was so much a part of her that she now realized she had recognized the box to be a magical object from the moment she had first set eyes on it.

"And a magic box," she said, "requires a magic key."

She thought of her uncle, and of all the spells and charms she had learned over the years as his apprentice. She thought of the Lights of Wonder spell he had taught her, and how Oona had used it to delight her mother and baby sister. And how the spell had gone so completely wrong, ending in their deaths.

And, of course, she thought of these last few days, when she had retained the hope that perhaps she had not been the cause of their deaths after all. It had been a false hope. Ridiculous, now that she thought of it. Oona had been there . . . had seen it all happen . . . and yet some part of her still clung to the thought that perhaps some other action, besides her own incompetence, had in the end caused the spell to go so wrong.

There are times when we humans open like a flower, our petals reaching outward for the answers we seek. But often, the answers that we are looking for are on the inside, and no reaching outward is necessary.

Oona shook her head, confused. Those had been her uncle's words from the day before. But why were they popping into her head now? She didn't even know what those words had meant.

But then another thought began to materialize in her head, one that was definitely related. It was an image of the Wizard standing in the Pendulum House front garden, the hedge clippers clasped in one hand, just before he had spoken those cryptic words. And then the curious occurrence with the rose. How beautiful it had been. The rose had opened to the Wizard's will. How truly . . .

Oona's head gave a little jerk. "The rose. The spell. Of course."

Remembering her empty pockets, it occurred to her how fortunate it was that the simple spell had not required a conductor.

Kneeling down, she placed the box in front of her and raised one finger, playing the memory of what had happened in the garden over in her mind. She closed her eyes, concentrating as thoroughly as she could, and uttered the words her uncle had spoken, hoping beyond hope that she remembered them correctly.

"Abra-ord-ion-all."

The box clicked.

Oona opened her eyes, her breath suddenly filled with excitement. The box remained on the floor in front of her, only now there appeared to be a seam running around the top portion—a very defined lid—and an intricate pattern of magical symbols materialized on the box as if they had been carved into the smooth surface. Carefully, delicately, Oona flipped the lid open, her hands shaky from the lingering effects of the spell. Beneath the lid lay what Oona recognized immediately as a magic wand. Beneath the wand was a small piece of metal embossed with the words *Property of Oswald*.

Oona gasped. "Is this what I think it is?"

"It is indeed," said a voice from behind her. It was not the voice of the architect. It was a voice that caused all the fine hairs along Oona's arms and neck to stand on end, a voice she would never be able to forget her whole life, even if she lived to be a hundred years old. At the sound of it, time seemed almost to stop, and her heart dropped sickeningly into her stomach. Could it be true, or had she simply imagined hearing it?

Oona jumped frantically to her feet, spinning around in a whirl of skirts, only to find Red Martin, the notorious criminal mastermind, standing ominously beside the architect, smiling his broad, malevolent smile at her.

CHAPTER EIGHTEEN

The Scoundrel's Plan

Dressed in a simple tan suit, Red Martin smiled a winning smile and extended his hand to Oona. Oona stepped back, cringing at the thought of being any closer to this horrible man who was not only responsible for most of the crime on Dark Street, but was also the man behind the murder of her father.

"Thank you, Miss Crate," he said with an air of false appreciation. "Thank you for opening that box for me. I've been trying to do it for more than five hundred years."

At first, the statement startled Oona, but then she remembered her own discovery from three months ago: how Red Martin had been using turlock root to keep himself the same age for hundreds of years.

"You?" Oona said, her voice trembling nervously. "How did you get up here?"

Red Martin continued to smile at her, though the smile came nowhere near his eyes.

"Where do you think I've been hiding all these months? Other than in Faerie, of course," he said. "What better place than here in my tower?" He gestured to a hidden door in the side of the pyramid. It hung open on its hinges, apparently leading to some hidden room beyond.

"*Your* tower?" Oona said dubiously.

Red Martin spread his hands wide. "Yes, mine. Who do you think has been designing and putting on this competition for the last half a millennium?"

Oona looked questioningly at the architect, her confusion growing more and more profound by the moment.

Red Martin began to chuckle. "Surely not this absurdly dressed man. Nor any previous so-called tower architects. They have all been hired men to play the part. Nothing more. The tower has been an instrument of my own, to find someone bright enough, and clever enough, to open that box."

He arrowed his finger at the box on the floor.

Oona suddenly recalled the achingly boring history lesson from the Museum of Magical History and began to understand. It all made a kind of bizarre sense. She stared at Red Martin in disbelief. "It was you . . . five hundred years ago. You were Bernard T. Slyhand, the painter who stole Oswald's wand."

Red Martin clapped his hands together, applauding. "Very good, Miss Crate. Slyhand was one of my many names. And yes, it was I who stole Oswald's wand all those centuries ago. But when I stole the wand, it was stuck inside the protective case that Oswald himself had made for it: that black box. I had no way of opening it. Nevertheless, I sent a ransom note to Oswald, along with a hurriedly painted portrait of the wand, in the hope that he would think I had managed to somehow open the box. But the painting was done purely from memory. Indeed, I have what is called an eidetic memory, which means that—"

"I know what it means," Oona said. "It means that you have the ability to remember any thing or event in perfect detail."

"Very good," said Red Martin. "I've never met anyone else with a memory to match my own. But I'm special in that way, I suppose."

"Don't flatter yourself," Oona said. "Sir Baltimore has an eidetic memory as well."

Red Martin grinned. "Well, at least he *thinks* he does."

Oona frowned, glancing nervously toward the outside door. She considered making a run for it. She might be able to get through the door before Red Martin or the architect could catch up to her, but where would she go from there? Her chest tightened as she fully realized her situation. She was trapped.

Red Martin pointed at the box. "Anyway, I created this contest to find someone smart enough to open that blasted thing. And here you are. I knew it would be you, Miss Crate. After five hundred years of waiting, I just knew it."

Oona turned to the architect, whom she now knew was not an architect at all, and said: "So you have been in league with Red Martin all along."

The little man shrugged apologetically. "It's good money. And it's more work than you might expect. Red Martin may have designed it, but I saw to its construction. I arranged the use of the carpets from the museum, and had the monkeys brought in from the World of Man. Not to mention reconstructing an entire riverboat."

"They are apes, not monkeys," Oona corrected.

"Whatever," the false architect said dismissively.

Red Martin rubbed his hands together, grinning like a schoolboy. "The flying snakes I smuggled in myself, from Faerie. I bred them right here in the tower."

Oona shook her head, realizing how stupid she had been not to have figured it out. Adler Iree had even brought the topic up after their wild ride with the flying serpents, but she had been too determined to win the challenge to give the matter much thought. And then, of course, it had slipped her mind.

"I should have known," she said.

Red Martin nodded his agreement. "You know, I had thought you might win at least *some* of the challenges. You did disappoint me there. And to think you nearly ruined everything trying to save that stupid Iree girl. I saw the two of you outside on the landing. She was about to fall, and you risked your own life to save her. I've never seen anything so foolish in my life. Why would you do such a thing? She was your enemy."

Oona slowly shook her head. "You'll never understand."

He shrugged. "You're probably right. But it does not matter. And now, the key to the Glass Gates is finally mine."

He moved to step around her, trying to get to the box.

Oona blocked his way. "You intend to use the wand to open the Glass Gates?"

Red Martin stopped less than a foot away, looking down at Oona as if he were truly surprised. "Why else would I want it? On the other side of those gates is Faerie. And while it is true, as you discovered for yourself, that I know a secret way through those gates, it is a miserably tedious task that takes weeks to smuggle my merchandise through."

"Merchandise?" Oona said, contemptuously. "You are undoubtedly responsible for smuggling across some of the most dangerous magical objects our world has ever known: objects that cause nothing but mischief, such as pixiewood poison and throttler's silk. Things that have no business leaving Faerie."

Red Martin cracked his knuckles. "I am a business-man. Where there is a demand, I provide the product."

"Ah, but only criminals and twisted individuals would want such terrible things," Oona said. "I know it must have been you who sent the silk to Mr. and Mrs. Dodger. Just because they owed you money? They might have died."

"It's not all bad," said Red Martin. "Why, just last month I managed to get hold of an entire carton of faerie crumb cake: a marvelously moist pastry dish, best served at room temperature, with molasses and warm milk. One swallow and you'll hear angels singing!"

Red Martin made a move to dart around Oona, but quick as a cat she snatched the wand from the box.

"I do not care about faerie crumb cake!" she shouted. "I care that you wish to use this wand as a convenience—to open and close the Glass Gates at your will, so that you can continue to deluge our world with your so-called merchandise. And you haven't given a thought to the fact that, the last time that those gates were open, the Queen of Faerie herself threatened to destroy every last living human in existence. Those gates are all that keep her army from passing through into this world, and then on to New York City, and the World of Man! Answer me this, Red Martin. With all of your customers dead, who will purchase your merchandise?"

Red Martin's eyelids drooped. "Don't be so naïve. You think I've been smuggling artifacts across the border for over five hundred years without being careful? I know my business, Miss Crate, and no little girl is going to get in my way." He looked her up and down. "In fact, I can think of one item in particular that I just might be able to get my hands on that would be of interest to you. With that key," he pointed at the wand, "I could slip over to Faerie in a jiffy and bring it back for you, as a kind of thank-you gift. I take it you have heard of the Punchbowl Oracle?"

Oona's eyes slitted. "It is a faerie tale, nothing more."

Red Martin grinned. "Yes, I know it is. And I know about Sir Baltimore's little scheme to distract you from the contest. I knew you would overcome such a blatant bit of misinformation. And of course I was right. But what would you say if I told you that there was an object that could actually do just what the punchbowl is supposed to, and give you a true answer to any question asked? It is called an Orb of Cathesis. Perhaps you've heard of them. They are very rare, even in Faerie. In fact, only ten have ever been known to exist. They work only once, and then their power is gone forever. I know just where I can get one. Let me have the wand, and I will fetch it for you. Whatever it is you wish so badly to know—that question that is burning away inside of you—you could learn the answer within a few hours. Just hand over the wand. Now that is a deal if I ever heard one. What do you say, Miss Crate?"

Oona winced, as if Red Martin had dealt her a physical blow. If what he was saying were true, she could find out once and for all what had happened that tragic day in the park nearly three years ago. To Oona's surprise, she found a part of her actually wanted to hand the wand over, wanted so badly to believe that, if she could learn the truth from this Orb of Cathesis, to know that she indeed was not responsible for the accident, then she would be able to put all of this confusion behind her. She would be free.

And yet another part of her—the much stronger, rational part of her personality—understood that whatever answer the orb gave, it would not bring her family back. It would not change the fact that they were gone. She knew that the orb could just as easily tell her that it *was* all her fault. She also understood that the only reason she was so caught up in this obsession to know the truth

271

was because some man had dressed up like a gypsy woman and simply said: "You are not responsible for the burden you hold."

For the second time in less than an hour, her uncle's words returned to her, filling up her thoughts like some magic spell conjured from the very back of her mind . . . only this time she thought she understood better what those words actually meant.

There are times when we humans open like a flower, our petals reaching outward for the answers we seek. But often, the answers that we are looking for are on the inside, and no reaching outward is necessary.

She swallowed a lump in her throat, her heartbeat quickening in her chest as the words meaning struck home. Regardless of what had actually happened, Oona had not *meant* for it to happen. She had loved her mother and her sister. She had meant only to please them. She knew this as an absolute fact: a fact that was more substantial and solid than any external bit of evidence could ever prove to her. No matter whether she was responsible for the accident or not, it did not change the fact that she had loved them, and still did.

The idea that she, Oona, would give the wand of the greatest magician of all time over to this scheming, manipulative, greedy scoundrel seemed all at once to be absurd. To believe that all he wanted the wand for was to slip through the Glass Gates from time to time was ridiculous. Even more of a joke was the thought that she could trust him to do anything he promised at all.

"I'm afraid you misjudged one little thing in your plot to get your hands on this wand," Oona said.

"And what is that?" Red Martin asked.

Oona's eyes flashed at him. "That if I could figure out how to open the box . . . then I would also be able to close it again."

Oona dropped to the floor.

Red Martin shouted. *"No!"*

He lunged, but too late. Oona's hand slammed the wand back into the box and closed the lid. As she did, she spoke the counterspell she had heard her uncle utter to the rose.

"Orx-ord-ion-ah."

The box sealed itself, once again becoming a solid piece of impenetrable wood. Red Martin grabbed for the box, but Oona leapt back, clutching the box in her arms. Red Martin was like a cat ready to pounce.

"I've read all of my father's old files on you, Red Martin," Oona said, keeping a steady distance. "Every detail he managed to put together. And if there is one thing that has always helped me sleep better at night, it was the fact that you seem to be incapable of performing magic yourself. You seem to rely completely on enchanted objects to perform any magical wrongdoing."

This seemed to touch a nerve with Red Martin. "What's your point?" he said, practically spitting the words.

"Well, if you want to open the Glass Gates, then you need this wand. If you want to hurt someone by magic, then you need to send them enchanted silk. But you, Red Martin, are incapable of performing magic on your own. In over five hundred years, you have never mastered it. And because of that, even if you manage to take this box from me, you will be unable to open it, even though you have just heard the spell with your own ears. You could say the spell a hundred times, and it would not open."

He grimaced at her. "You speak truly. But there's one thing you have forgotten."

Oona felt a stab of panic. "And what would that be?"

"I can always force someone to do it for me. Someone who *can* do magic. Let me show you what I mean."

His hand dipped into the pocket of his jacket, and an instant later he brought it out again, holding what appeared to be some kind of finely crafted chain-mail glove. He quickly slipped the glove over his hand and flexed his fingers.

Oona eyed it mistrustfully. She did not know what it was, but, judging from Red Martin's pleased expression, it could not be good for her.

"Ah. Admiring my new glove, are you, Miss Crate?" he said. "It is faerie-made armor. Impervious to magic. You see, unlike some people, I learn from my mistakes. So you might want to think twice before trying your little *Switch* spell on me this time. It won't work."

Oona shook her head, not understanding. Why would she wish to use the *Switch* spell? He did not hold anything she wished to have. But an instant later she understood all too well what Red Martin had meant as he dipped the gloved hand into his pocket and brought it out again, this time holding a revolver.

Oona's heart skipped a beat. Many criminals carried guns, she knew—a bullet through the heart had killed her father—but she had never faced a gun before, and she was terrified. She realized her mistake in having closed the wand back in the box. Had she not done so, she might have used it to defend herself. Now it was too late. Red Martin leveled the revolver, and Oona hesitated, unsure if she should believe him about the glove or not.

As if reading her thoughts, Red Martin's grin widened. "Go ahead, try it."

She tightened her grip on the wand box, unsure of what to do. The last time Oona had been in such a situation, she had used Samuligan's *Switch* command to magically exchange Red Martin's dagger with her own candlestick, but if what he was saying was true, then the spell would not be able to work on his revolver hand.

She considered doing as he had suggested, and trying it anyway, but reason stopped her. Even if he was lying about the faerie armor, and she did attempt the spell, she would only be giving Red Martin exactly what he wanted: the box. Then of course she would have the gun. But if what he was saying was true, and the glove did block the spell, then there was the possibility that the box in *her* hand might still be affected by the spell while the gun in *his* hand was not. If that were the case, then by uttering the magical command, she might actually send the box to Red Martin without receiving anything in return. He would have the box and the gun, and she would have nothing.

Or perhaps there is some other variation I'm not even thinking of, she thought. It was all so infuriatingly complicated, and this was one of the reasons that Oona disliked the fickleness of magic. There were so many possibilities to consider.

"Enough!" Red Martin shouted. "Speak the spell and hand the box over now, Miss Crate, or I will shoot you. And don't try to grab the wand from the box. You may be fast, but not *that* fast."

Oona swallowed hard. There appeared to be no other option. Though he seemed reluctant simply to shoot her and have it done with, Oona knew that if she gave him good reason, Red Martin would have no qualms against pulling the trigger.

Three months earlier he had set two of his muscle men with clubs on Deacon and her. Oona had detained them by using *Lux lucis admiratio*, the Lights of Wonder . . . but that difficult spell required a conductor to focus the energy in a single direction, like a stick or a wand—or, in the case of the thugs, a broken chair leg.

Her pockets she knew were empty, and her only option at present was to use the box in her hand, but its shape was not optimal. The spell was highly unpredictable, and without a proper conductor to focus the energy, it might shoot off in just about any direction, maybe even hitting herself, or prompting Red Martin to fire the gun.

No, what she needed was the wand that was inside the box—or a spell that did not require a conductor.

Red Martin appeared to have read her mind. "What, no magic to help you, Miss Crate?"

Oona glanced at the floor, and the idea came to her in a flash. If it didn't work, then she knew all was lost, but at the moment she saw no alternative. She had to be quick. "You're right, Red Martin," she said, doing her best to sound defeated. "You have won."

Red Martin's face split in a terrible grin. "I know I have. Now open the box, and bring it here."

Oona raised one finger, tapping the side of the box. *"Abra-ord-ion-all."*

Once again the seam appeared in the box, creating the outline of a lid.

"Here." She set the box on the floor at her feet and stepped away. "Come and get it."

This was it, the moment of truth. Oona's stomach seemed to contract as Red Martin stepped forward, eyes fixed on the box, gun dropping to his side. What he failed to notice, however, was that, as he moved across the room, straight in front of him was the large X painted on the floor. The instant he placed his foot down, Oona dropped to her knees and tapped her finger against the floor.

"Abra-ord-ion-all!"

The trapdoor snapped open. A shout leapt from Red Martin's throat that followed him as he disappeared through the hole in the floor. Oona quickly snatched the wand from the box and aimed it at the architect. His eyes shifted nervously in their sockets.

"You're next," she said, pointing to the trapdoor.

The phony architect frowned. "Do I have to?"

Oona gave the wand a jabbing motion. "Do it, or I'll turn you into a worm."

Oona knew very well that she had no such power, but the architect certainly did not. He let out a small whimper, and then dropped through the trapdoor opening. Oona peered over the lip of the trapdoor, watching him slide until he was out of view.

She took a moment to collect herself, peering at the powerful magical object in her hand, and realized all at once that the last person to hold this wand had been Oswald the Great himself. What great and terrible powers this wand had conjured; it made her nervous simply to hold it.

At last, still feeling thoroughly shaken, Oona retrieved the box from the floor and tucked it beneath her arm. Her hands trembled as she allowed herself a sigh of relief. She was alive, and Red Martin's plans had been thwarted. She could only hope that the spectators waiting below would see him emerge from the slide at the bottom of the tower. Reminding herself that the man still had a gun, her heart lurched at the thought of someone attempting to apprehend him and getting shot in the bargain.

Glancing down at the open trapdoor, she said: "Well, I'm certainly not going down that way."

She had a better idea.

CHAPTER NINETEEN

The Kiss

D eorsum tardus!"

Oona tapped the rope at the top of the elevator cage with the tip of Oswald's wand, and she and the cage began to descend. The ride down was quite slow, but Oona was afraid that if she made the rickety elevator travel any faster, its rope might come loose or break altogether.

The rain had receded to a slow drizzle, and Oona was thankful for it; but as the park drew closer and the spectators became larger, Oona began to feel quite anxious. What would she find when she got down there? Would anyone have tried to apprehend Red Martin? Would they have succeeded? She had not heard a gunshot, but then again she had been very high up and might not have heard the explosion from so far away.

Deacon was the first to see her as the cage came level with the tops of the trees. He flew to the top of the cage and looked from the wand in her right hand to the black box in her left.

He shook the water excitedly from his wings. "You did it! You solved the puzzle box. You've won!"

Oona looked urgently around. "Where is Red Martin? And the architect?"

"Red Martin?" Deacon asked.

"Yes, Deacon. Didn't you see him come out of the slide? And the architect, too."

Deacon shook his head. "I'm not sure what you are speaking of, but we haven't seen either of them."

Oona scanned the spectators below. Deacon was right. There was no sign of the architect or Red Martin. Not that she thought they would have stayed nearby, but she didn't understand why no one saw them.

The cage came to a halt on the stage. A round of applause emanated from the sparse crowd, but Oona hardly noticed. She spotted Isadora Iree beside her mother near the front of the stage. She stood, arms crossed, refusing to applaud with the others. Oona strode swiftly across the stage to meet her.

"Come to gloat?" Isadora asked sulkily.

Oona shook her head. "Isadora, where did you come out of the tower?"

The question seemed to take Isadora by surprise. "What?"

"The slide," Oona said. "Where does the slide come out?"

Isadora squinched up her nose at the memory. "Oh, that? It was just horrible. I thought I was going to die, swirling around and around like that. It made me quite dizzy, and I thought I might be sick."

Oona looked impatiently around. "But where did it come out?"

Isadora waived a hand vaguely toward the tower. "Through a hole at the back."

Oona turned to her uncle and Samuligan, who stood near the steps to the stage. She snapped her fingers. "Quickly. To the back of the tower!"

She descended the steps in a single bound and began hurriedly making her way around the side of the building.

"What is it, Oona dear?" the Wizard asked, struggling to keep up with her.

Deacon landed on her shoulder. "Yes, where are we going?"

Oona glanced back, happy to see that Samuligan was following closely behind.

"It's Red Martin," she said. "He's been living at the

top of the tower. He went down the slide . . . and he has a gun."

Before she could round the back corner, a hand grabbed her arm, stopping her in her tracks. It was her uncle.

"A gun?" he asked. "Are you sure?"

She gave him a peeved look. "Of course I'm sure. Red Martin has been behind this tower competition all along. That architect wasn't an architect after all. He was just a phony whom Red Martin paid to play the part. They used me to open the box and get this." Oona held up the wand. "Oswald's wand."

The Wizard's eyes rounded in surprise. "Oswald's original wand?"

"Yes," Oona said. She glanced at the box beneath her arm. "This is what was in the puzzle box. But there's no time to explain. We mustn't let Red Martin get away."

She turned, intent on heading around the corner, but the Wizard's hand prevented her from moving forward.

"Oona, stop," he said. "Think. If he has a gun . . ."

"But we can't let him get away," she said, and her voice broke with emotion. "He killed my father!"

"But he has a gun," the Wizard repeated.

She felt like her head might explode with frustration, and she bit at her lip, holding back a retort. She knew her uncle was right. Not only did Red Martin have a gun, but also a glove that could repel magic. She could think of no one more dangerous.

"Why don't I take a look?" Deacon suggested. "I can fly to that tree over there."

"An excellent idea," the Wizard said.

Oona glanced sideways at Deacon. "Be careful."

"Without a doubt," he replied, and then soared into the air.

They watched him circle high in the air and land in the tree. His head twitched this way and that, peering in all directions behind the tower. At last he called to them.

"I don't see them anywhere. Neither the architect nor Red Martin."

Samuligan tipped his hat back on his head before poking his faerie face around the corner of the building. At last he stepped forward. "All seems clear."

Oona and the Wizard stepped around the corner. The end of the slide stuck out of a hole in the building like a long, flat tongue. Red Martin and his minion were nowhere to be seen.

"Where could they have gone?" Oona asked.

The park was enormous, nearly a mile long and a quarter mile deep. But still. Someone must have seen them.

"Unless . . . ," Oona said, and ran to the end of the slide. "Look."

Several paces from the end of the slide a green gas lamppost stood forlornly against the drab, gray sky. Many of the street's lamps had not yet been converted to the Wizard's ever-burning lamplight, and here was one of them. She approached the post, but stopped several feet away and looked down. At her feet she found a thick, round piece of iron, approximately three feet across, set into the grass: the letters UH were embossed on top.

"A utility-hole cover," Deacon said.

Oona nodded. "Yes. It leads down to underground passages where the utility workers can work on the gas lines. I know about them from my father's files. He believed that all sorts of criminal activity happened down in those tunnels." She knelt. "And see here, how the wet grass is flat on this side of the hole? This is where the cover was recently moved so someone could crawl inside before sliding the lid back into place."

"Or two people," Deacon reasoned.

"Yes," Oona said, straightening her knees. "The false architect . . . and Red Martin. He has managed to escape once again."

Oona's shoulders slumped. It was simply intolerable to know that her father's murderer was still at large.

"But look at what you have, Oona," the Wizard said, and there was a hint of reverence in his voice. "You have Oswald the Great's wand, and Red Martin does not."

Samuligan leaned down to get a better look at the wand. Oona could not read his expression, and yet, suddenly, something occurred to her.

"This is the very wand used to turn you into a life-long servant of Pendulum House, isn't it, Samuligan?"

He nodded, his expression still unreadable. "It is one of them. Oswald did not act alone."

But still, Oona wondered if this wand might be the key to setting Samuligan free. It was, after all, rumored to be the key to the Glass Gates. It just might be the way to send the faerie home.

She thought of how sad that would make her. Samuligan was like family. How empty the house would seem without him.

The faerie servant, who sometimes gave the impression that he could read thoughts, straightened beside her, and said: "It is an interesting find, indeed."

The Wizard cleared his throat. "Now, Oona dear, you must tell us everything that you have learned."

As the four of them wound their way back around to the front of the tower, Oona recounted all that had happened in the pyramid. She was in the middle of explaining how pompous and arrogant Red Martin had been acting—boasting of how cleverly he had been to steal the wand box five hundred years ago, and how he had used his eidetic memory to paint a picture of the wand locked inside—when Oona suddenly stopped.

They had just come around the front side of the tower to where the spectators remained, scattered sparsely around the stage. Perhaps they were all waiting to find out what had happened, Oona wasn't sure. But one realization suddenly did jump into her mind that she could not believe she had not seen before.

Oona marched across the wet grounds and arrowed a finger at Sir Baltimore. "You, sir, are the reason Isadora Iree was able to cheat her way through the contest!"

"Me?" Sir Baltimore said. "I haven't the slightest idea what you are—"

"Not only did you hire that phony fortune-teller to distract me with a faerie tale," Oona said, "but you were also the one who stole the plans from the architect the night of the party. And this is how it happened." Oona turned to Madame Iree. "You, madame, purposely ran into the architect so that he would spill his soup on your dress."

"Why would she do that?" Deacon asked.

Oona peered hard at Madame Iree. "She did it because Mrs. White, the wife of our very own Inspector White, was wearing a similar dress."

Madame Iree opened and closed her mouth several times before saying: "It was horrible. I couldn't stand the humiliation of being the most celebrated dressmaker on the street and attending a party with someone in a similar dress."

"So instead," Oona continued, "you suffered the humiliation of having your own dress soiled with soup, so you could then have an excuse to run back to your dress shop for a change of wardrobe."

Madame Iree looked at her daughter, and the two of them nodded as if this were a perfectly reasonable thing to do.

"Originality is very important," said Madame Iree.

"But what does that have to do with Sir Baltimore?" Deacon asked.

"I was just getting to that," Oona said, returning her attention to Roderick's tall, handsome father. "You, sir, were in the group of people who rushed to help the architect back to his feet after he and Madame Iree collided, and in all that commotion, you saw your chance and took it. You slyly unbuckled the architect's satchel and removed the papers. You then used your eidetic memory to take a mental picture of the plans, memorizing all the clues and their answers in the few minutes that they went missing. In the chaos caused by the incident, no one would have noticed you, and even if someone had, I'm guessing that you used Penelope's book of obscure faerie tales to hide the plans from view as you glanced them over.

Once you'd finished, you then dropped the plans on the ground, where they were soon found by Deacon. You later gave the answers to Roderick and placed a large bet on him to win. Of course, what you did not know was that the final clue in the plans was false."

Isadora Iree stood between her mother and her boyfriend. Her hair and dress were as wet as ever. Presently, she slapped Roderick on the shoulder. "You told me the final answer was 'rutabaga'!"

"Hush, Isadora," Roderick said, his face going just as red as his father's.

"Isadora?" Madame Iree said. "You were cheating this whole time? I simply don't believe it."

Isadora's mouth clamped shut, and she gazed up at her mother with large innocent eyes.

Adler, who was leaning on a nearby tree, gave a quick disbelieving laugh. "Ha! So those notes that Roderick was giving you . . . They weren't love poems after all, were they, sister? They were the answers to the contest clues."

Isadora scowled at Adler.

"So, that's it, Roderick?" Sir Baltimore said through gritted teeth. He turned abruptly on his son, pointing his finger menacingly. "You were giving all the answers I gave to you to your girlfriend? And here I thought you were just incompetent, but apparently, I should change that to stupid."

Roderick pulled himself up straight. "Chivalry! Chivalry! Chivalry!"

"Balderdash!" said Sir Baltimore. "Do you realize how much money you've lost me?"

Roderick sneered at his father. "Well, maybe I would have won after all, if that *supposedly* perfect memory of yours wasn't so faulty. You couldn't even remember what the plans said about the flying carpets and how to get them to work. And all those clocks yesterday. You forgot which ones were real and which were false. I had to figure that out myself!"

"Imagine that," Oona said.

"We're going home!" Sir Baltimore declared, before marching off in the direction of the park entrance. "Roderick! Penelope!"

"I want a story!" Penelope cried as she followed hurriedly after her father. "The one about the Punchbowl Oracle!"

Sir Baltimore cringed at the mention of the bowl and suddenly began to walk faster. Roderick bent to kiss Isadora's hand, but Isadora jerked away and stalked off across the park toward the exit, Roderick following closely behind like a scolded puppy dog.

"But, my lady," he tried to reason with her, "there was no way I could have known about the final question. I simply could not have . . ."

His voice trailed off as he moved out of earshot, and the rest of the crowd began to disperse.

The Wizard extended a hand to Oona. "May I see the wand, Oona?" he asked.

Oona handed over the wand and the box. The Wizard turned the wand in his long, wrinkled fingers. "Come, let us take this back to Pendulum House, for safekeeping . . . and of course, to celebrate."

"Celebrate what?" Oona asked, feeling that Red Martin's escape was no reason to rejoice.

"To celebrate your victory," said Adler. The boy stepped forward, tipping his top hat back on his head. "After all, you are the first person ever to solve all the levels and every clue of the Magician's Tower."

"A party is in order," said the Wizard, looking suddenly not like an old man, but like a child who had just received precisely what he wanted for a birthday present. "Samuligan, we have arrangements to make."

Samuligan nodded, and the two of them turned in the direction of the park entrance. Oona saw the Wizard give a little skip as he and Samuligan crossed the park, and Samuligan began to whistle a tune so eerily sweet that several crows ventured from their nests to flutter about his cowboy hat.

Oona turn to Adler, meaning to ask if he would care to accompany them back to Pendulum House, when the boy leaned forward and kissed her. A wave of electricity shot through her, strong and fierce. It was her very first kiss.

Deacon squawked and flew from her shoulder, landing on a high branch.

"Oh," she said as Adler straightened. "You startled Deacon." She did not add that she herself had been startled, though in a very good way. She tilted her head coyly. "What was that for?"

Adler shrugged, grinning broadly. "'Cause I wanted to."

Oona glanced quickly around to see if anyone was watching. Deacon was perched in a tree, high above, his back to them as if something enormously interesting were happening across the street.

The fact that the kiss had happened here, on the very spot where the accident had occurred so many years ago, was not lost on Oona. For the briefest of moments she felt the chilly fingers of guilt wrap around her insides, threatening to tug her downward, intent on spoiling the moment. But before the guilt could take hold completely, another thought sprang into her mind, and the uneasy feeling disappeared.

Abra-ord-ion-all, she thought.

Oona took Adler's hand and squeezed. Her heart was racing, and all at once she felt incredibly daring. Before she could stop herself, she stood boldly on her tiptoes and kissed Adler on the cheek. Adler blushed, and the electric sensation shot through Oona once again. It was a familiar feeling, she realized, one she'd known her entire life.

It was just like magic.